AVARICE

G. K. LUND

Northern
Quill Press

Published by Northern Quill Press.

ISBN: 978-82-93663-11-9

https://gklundwrites.com

Cover design by Damonza.

Edited by Megan Easley-Walsh and N. Hall.

Avarice/G.K. Lund, 1st. ed.

"When the evil spirit has once taken hold of the heart of man, it urges him on, without letting him stop."

Alexandre Dumas
The Black Tulip

Amsterdam, January 1637

The precious cargo of beautiful and expensive textiles was presumed to have gone down with the ship. It was either the Spanish or an unforeseen natural event that had sent the three-master to the desolate dark depths of the ocean. A magnificent vessel of human ingenuity destroyed. A cargo of the best silk now lost and rotting away, eaten by the tiny creatures of the seabed, not to be of use to anyone.

Willem de Meer had heard about this likely event from his father on what would be the day that changed his life for the worse; though not for the first time. Nothing could ever be the same after this, but then again — it hadn't been for a long time already. He stared through the small and barred window on the ground floor in his father's warehouse, close to the harbor. The canal outside would not facilitate any merchandise from *The Filomena* to be brought there. Not now. Willem watched people walking past the building in their ignorant bliss, going about their normal day. Barrels were rolled by, dogs barked, a fishmonger shouted as he walked past while announcing his wares. The fishy smell seeped in through the large doors that were left ajar. It was such a lovely day. Cold, yes. It bit the skin, but the sun was out. Every person that passed Willem's gaze had ruddy cheeks and looked splendid in their wholesomeness.

"Wim?" His father's voice came behind him. He had given him a moment to gather his thoughts. Willem blinked. No thoughts were really gathered, were they?

"Wim?" his father repeated. His stern raised voice caused a coughing fit to overtake him, and Willem pulled away from the window as he ran to his father's side.

"Father, here, sit down a moment," he said as he helped the older man sit on a nearby empty barrel as he put the lid on it so his father could rest. "De Vries, water," he added to his father's servant who had not gotten there first. Willem noticed the dark and lanky man's hesitation at his order, but he would not refuse his master water.

His father's coughing went on for several minutes, and the sight of this was worse to comprehend for Willem than the news he had received already. He had never seen the man this way before. He wore fine clothing: expensive fabrics formed into his shirt, jerkin, ruffled cuffs and white collar. It all spoke of wealth, but it was also nothing more than remnants now. Pieter de Meer had always been strong, been in charge and settled anything that needed a firm hand and strong will to be dealt with. To Willem, he had always looked the same, but today he realized he had never paid any attention to the signs of age in his father. The graying hair, the lines in his soft yet marked face that had become more defined and deeper. The pale skin and the blue eyes that were not as sharp anymore. It dawned on Willem that looking into this face was like looking into the future, for he resembled his father. Though at twenty-two his face had no lines yet, and his hair was a deep dark brown and would remain so for years to come.

"Here you are, Mynheer," De Vries said as he handed his master a glass filled with water. Pieter took it and drank, and it was clear the liquid soothed his aching throat.

"Don't you have something stronger?" he asked when he regained his voice.

"I think there is some brandy left in the office."

"That'll do."

"Are you sick, Father?" Willem asked as he heard De Vries' steps going upstairs to the small private office that was not used to greet customers.

"I'll be fine, Son. We have more grave matters than this to deal with." The old man waved him off.

Willem was not so sure. He had never seen the man like this before. Granted, Willem did not spend much time at home, what with his studies these days, but he had not seen any signs of sickness a couple of months ago. Perhaps his father calling him back to Amsterdam in such a rush should have tipped him off. He should have seen that something was wrong, but the thought had not even occurred to him. He had left at once when the letter from his father arrived and traveled from Leiden as quickly as he could, for it had told him to make haste. He was beginning to see why. The warehouse around him was, for the most part, empty. There was nothing on the shelves, empty barrels all around. No employees. Only a barren building that echoed their words from the naked walls, and smelled of...nothing. Willem remembered being allowed in here as a boy. The dry smell of the textiles, the sharp smells of dyed fabric that would still linger. It was his father's preferred merchandise, something people always needed, something he understood. And now, this stubborn focus on only one type of merchandise was turning on them.

"Tell me what happened."

"As I said," his father began before he stopped himself. He coughed again and drank of the water before De Vries returned and switched the glasses in his master's hand. The brandy went down better and did the same trick as the water. "I have waited and waited for *The Filomena* to return, but must now resign myself to the truth. She must have gone down somewhere along her route."

"Maybe she has been derailed from her course somehow? She set sail late. Winter storms can be hard to predict."

Pieter shook his head slowly.

"No. *The Silver Wind* sailed three weeks later, and that crew came sailing into the harbor two weeks ago. She is lost to us."

"Surely you have other stakes on other ships?"

"I did, but misfortune has befallen them all. The Spanish, pirates, Mother Nature. It is all out of my hands now."

"How bad is it?"

"My fortune is almost gone. I have only scraps left. I have sold off the house in Haarlem, to keep things going and pay the last wages. I have let most of our staff and servants go."

Willem glanced up at De Vries at this. The servant had been there as long as he could remember. Willem didn't know much but he had picked up a few things over the years. From what he understood, his father and De Vries had fought in the war together. The loyalty of De Vries could only have come from his life being saved by his employer. Of course, the last part was Willem's guess, but nothing else made sense to him.

"De Vries is loyal," Pieter said, noting his son's look. "He will stay to the end."

De Vries nodded at this, his dark eyes revealing his agreement as the rest of his bony and angular face remained passive. His face was not a particularly animated one, but that did not mean he didn't express his opinion when he deemed it necessary. It made Willem cringe to think about.

"The end?" Willem repeated. "Surely it's not that bad?"

"It is. I'm afraid your studies will have to wait as well, Son. I can no longer afford them." Willem had gone off to university at his father's request more than any wish he'd had himself, but he had come to like it more than expected. Perhaps that had been because of his brother Geert. He had made everything an adventure. Willem had hoped to one day become a lawyer. It would have been a good way to help his father and brother. That didn't seem like a viable option now. It had to be less than an hour since he hastened into his father's warehouse, and already what little was left of any meaning was crumbling in front of him. Everything he had ever counted on and taken for granted was disappearing. In his mind's eye, he saw the blue silk melding into the dark waters. He saw brocade falling apart and silver threads that would never glint in the sunshine, as light would never again reach it. All of it lost, and for nothing.

There was silence between them for a moment. Only the voices and occasional shouts from the street outside could be heard. Someone was selling, someone laughing at a joke or grandiose compliment. A dog barked, and something splashed into the canal followed by a curse and abruptly quieted language.

Willem felt an ache in his right knee as he had been kneeling his leg on the hard wooden-floor for too long. He got to his feet and inhaled sharply, only a smell of newly gathered dust to be noticed.

"All right. What can I do?"

His father looked up at him, a small smile at the word 'I'. An almost imperceptible snort escaped De Vries at the same time, and Willem attempted to ignore him. He was never supposed to take over his father's business. No, that had been Geert's burden. His brother had encompassed his father's sense of business, his knowledge, and a likable demeanor. His father could never be run out of business by scammers and flawed deals, but the acts of nature? That was something else. A drunken night had ended all that was Geert, and Willem had to force that thought away. He had to do what Geert could no longer do.

"I have one last resort," his father said and took a sip of the brandy again. "I didn't have much left, but most of it went into a good bargain. If acted upon, it can bring us a good return on our investment."

Willem could not help the hopeful smile on his face at this. His father always knew what he was doing.

"What is it? Did you strike a deal with one of the other merchants?" The De Meer name was a good and trusted name in Amsterdam; surely his father had managed a decent deal on account of that.

"Revealing our misfortune would mean sullying our name. No, I invested the money in the *Magna Avaritia*."

Willem stared at him a moment, then at De Vries, but there was no help to be found there. Then it dawned on him what his father had actually said.

"The *Magna Avaritia?*" he repeated. "Bulbs? You invested it all in a tulip?"

2

"You never bought into the tulip market," Willem insisted while keeping his voice low. They had left the warehouse as his father insisted the fresh air was better for him. So, they had donned their fur-trimmed and wool-lined cloaks. Their broad-brimmed hats shielded their eyes from the sun. There was no snow, but the frozen ground crunched under their feet as they headed towards the harbor. Ships being loaded and unloaded met them, a frenzied yet controlled environment of efficient men working hard. People were walking to and fro; some met sailors they had not seen in months. Others purchased various goods from vendors who screamed for the attention of any heavy purse.

"You said it was too uncertain for your taste," Willem pressed on. De Vries kept a few paces behind them, as he always did when his father was accompanied by someone.

"It is, but as our situation has changed so radically, I had no choice."

"But, Father...it's not stable like the textile business. You have always said so."

"If I'm right about this, we can make back seven or

eight times my investment. It may even be more. That would be enough to get us going again."

"But... tulip speculation?" Willem shook his head. Many a citizen had made fortunes on the beautiful flowers, but he had always listened to his father. Keep to what's safe. He had always done so, except for the one time when, in a drunken stupor, a couple of Willem's fellow students had lured him into a tulip bargain. He had spent the few Florins he had and luckily made a nice little profit. It had not made him rich in his own right, but it had saved him from begging his father for more allowance. He had been damn lucky, and he had never even seen the flower, only the bulb. Apparently, that particular tulip was supposed to be the most radiant yellow. He had never told his father of this near mistake, and he was not going to now. It gave him shivers to think about under his winter attire. There was so much more at stake now.

"It's the only option left to us," his father insisted as they neared a beggar woman seated by a large six-story warehouse. She never caused any problems and the owner left her to herself out there, instead of having her chased away. Willem waited for his father to break step as usual, and then he realized he wasn't going to. Willem walked over to her, as he fished a coin out of his purse.

"Hello, Annetje," he said as the woman looked up at him. "I hope you're keeping warm." He had no idea how old she was, but much like De Vries, she had always been there as well. She looked wrinkled and tired, maybe in her forties? There was no way of telling. She was always wearing thick layers of clothes, concealing everything but her weathered face, even in summer.

"I am. Bless you, Mynheer de Meer," she said as he put the coin in her little bowl.

"You might want to start thinking about what you do

with your money now, don't you think?" his father said with reproach as Willem came back.

He bent his head a little. His father was right of course. It was irresponsible to pretend he had money now. He slowed down his gait to match that of his father and they continued on.

"I made the deal with a grower outside the city. I have signed the contract he sent me and need you to—"

"Pieter," a shrill voice broke through whatever it was Willem was supposed to do.

"Ah, Little Pieter," his father said at the sight of his cousin approaching them. He was a big man with a round waist, too fond of the fine foods and his own wine. His blond hair came from a different side of the family, his happy and boasting disposition as well. Willem knew his father had always enjoyed the fact that Little Pieter was the younger of the two, so he could call him that to his dying day. They both shared their grandfather's name.

"And young Wim," Little Pieter said at the sight of Willem. "I haven't seen you in a long time. How are your studies going?"

Willem had to wait to answer as a group of younger Little-Pieter-offspring came up to their father and joined him. He'd broken away from them at the sight of his cousin. Pieter van Linden was a wine merchant, opting for something people wanted, not needed like Pieter de Meer had done. It struck Willem as strange how that difference had happened. He noticed the weakness in his father as they chatted with their kin and how he struggled to look like the forceful personality he had always been. Now, Little Pieter seemed to dominate the conversation.

"I heard *The Filomena* hasn't returned yet," he said as the eventual small talk and updated family information had been seen to. Willem found he had no patience for his relatives' forays into education as well as getting experience in their father's business. It did not strike him as important in the midst of his own father's struggle.

"It has not," Pieter answered in truth.

"Well, mayhap she'll turn up one of these days." The smile on Little Pieter's face seemed ever-present and an insult, though Willem thought that might not be the case. He knew there had always been competition between the cousins, but that didn't make them enemies.

"I think not," Pieter answered him, his voice curt.

"So how are things going? If you have any gold thread, I know my Maria is in need of it."

"That was supposed to arrive with *The Filomena*, so it is the one thing I do not have in stock."

Both Willem and De Vries kept silent at this blatant lie. It was clear Pieter did not want to share any information regarding his demise with his cousin. Nor did they feel any inclination to do so.

"Ah, well," Little Pieter said and then couldn't stop himself from playing around the fire. "Perhaps you should venture into the tulip speculation? It has brought me good fortune in addition to the red, liquid gold, of course. I have invested in the most lustrous *couleren* myself, the *Admirael de Baas*. It should fetch a Florin or two come the season, I should think. Or sooner." He gave a conspiratorial wink at that.

"A good deal, I'm sure," Pieter said and left it at that. At least his cousin took the hint, and excused himself, still with his smile. *The Nefertiti* had entered the harbor at dawn, filled with the most exquisite wines from God-knows-where. And oh, he would send some over to his beloved cousin of course. And naturally, Maria would have her golden threads as soon as they were again in stock.

Willem watched this exchange in a well-hidden puzzlement, for he dared not reveal any of his father's lies for what they were. He honestly didn't begrudge him his pride. It had gotten him so far in life already.

"He knows," Pieter hissed and then began coughing again as soon as Little Pieter and his brood were so far away they mingled into the crowd on the wharf.

"What? How?"

"His tulip. The *Admirael de Baas*. That's the name of the cultivator. I am buying the *Magna Avaritia* from him," Pieter gave in to his coughing then and could say no more. Willem turned to De Vries. He always knew everything. He was always there when his father conducted his business.

"There has been some rift to close the deal on the *Magna Avaritia*," De Vries explained when Willem asked. The servant's tone indicated he should have understood this simple fact on his own. "It is not unlikely that Van Linden was in negotiations to buy the bulb. The bidding has been going on ever since the season ended. And so, he likely knows that your father has suddenly gone into a business he has so far stayed out of."

"He knows," Pieter said with conviction as the coughing ceased, and his pride was pushed further towards the abyss.

Willem pressed his lips together and nodded hard, dipping his chin once.

"All right. Tell me about these bulbs."

"It will be a most spectacular flower when it blooms. It is a *violetten*, one of the rare-striped beauties. It is a pure white with streaks of a purple so dark it is almost black. It will be a beauty few others can match. The *Admirael van Baas* will be of no contest in artistry by the cultivator's own admission."

Willem did not argue. There was no point at this stage, and he never did argue with his father anyway. The money was spent, and by the sound of it, he had spent more than Willem had thought while in the warehouse. His father must have gambled everything on this one flower to get the contract for it. Likely he had outbid others for cheaper and still expensive bulbs that could also have gotten them through this crisis. It was done, and all Willem could do was help. To help like he had failed to when it came to Geert, his father's true and just hope for the future.

"I have the contract, signed and ready, and I have the payment, but I cannot send De Vries. Van Baas will only deal directly with me or a family member."

"That leaves you," De Vries said, a wry smile on his face.

Willem ignored him and focused on his ailing father.

"Obviously you can't go, Father."

"I agree. It's not far, just outside the city. But I don't think I can manage."

"Don't worry. Of course, I will do this for you." Willem meant it. He would do anything to help his father. Pieter de Meer might be a strict and strong-willed man, but what were you if you couldn't protect those you loved? It seemed, only for this short time, that the roles had changed on young Willem and his father.

3

Willem walked through the house with trepidation. Everything in there reminded him of Geert. The paintings on the walls they had made up stories about. The checkered floors where they had skipped, losing the game if their feet touched the lines. The elegant furniture that they had been forced to sit properly on. They had then raced between it and jumped on it when their parents or servants had been occupied elsewhere. Now the house seemed as dead as his brother in its darkened state. The tinted glass did nothing to help, nor the near darkness outside. A few lamps were lit, but as he walked through the rooms he knew he was in a house that no longer lived. It was Geert and their mother that had brought joy inside these walls. The bustle of the servants as well. Now, as far as he knew, only old Hendrika remained. She had not been there when he entered the house after having left his father and De Vries at the harbor to return to the house on the Keizersgracht. His father insisted that Willem should make haste and procure the bulb. Not until it was in their hands, could they be assured of a profit. So many deals were made every day in the taverns, often without buyers even seeing their flowers. To sell this tulip though, the *Magna Avaritia*, new and already famed, they needed to prove they had it. Willem shook his head as he headed further into the house, towards the kitchen. The whole country had been gripped by this mania, and now it seemed his father had finally given in as well. Pieter de Meer, a tulipomaniac? No, Willem reminded himself as he saw light ahead coming from the kitchen, his father was no true tulip speculant. His situation was dire, and this was a one-time means to an end. Would it even have come to this if Geert had been here? Perhaps his father was too stricken with grief to manage as he had before.

Tobacco smoke hit him before he entered the kitchen and saw old Hendrika seated at the table smoking her long-stemmed, clay pipe. It had always been her treat after a long working day. Willem could remember Geert and himself coming in here when they were boys, eyes wide at the smoking woman.

"Master Willem," she said and stood. He could hear her old bones creaking all the way to the door.

"Hendrika. Good to see you."

"I'm sorry. I didn't hear the door."

He shook his head. He did have a key after all.

"I have business to do for my father, but I hoped to see if you had something to eat first."

That got the old woman going as she scrounged up a quick dinner for him. His father had told her not to cook that day as he would not be coming back until late, so Willem dined on cold meats and stewed vegetables from the day before. *It matters little*, he thought as he wolfed it down; starving after his travels and bad news. He should be thankful he had anything to eat now, shouldn't he?

He was almost done as he heard Hendrika shuffling into the dining room, the smell of tobacco accompanying her.

"Pardon, Master Willem, but there is someone at the

door." The look she bore puzzled him. It was not particularly late.

"Who is it?"

"It is Miss van Heuvel."

Willem swallowed down a particularly chewy piece of carrot.

"Here?"

"Yes. And she is unaccompanied."

Willem gave a mental eye roll at that but was still worried. He had forgotten about Catharijn. He did not think too much about her at all. What could she want, and only a few hours after he came back to the city?

He went into the Green Parlor where Hendrika had shown the young lady. The room had been given the name as Willem's mother had loved the color. The furniture donned a deep-sea green, the dark wood contrasting it. No painting had been hung in there without a dominant presence of green or silver and the tinted windows bore strong signs of it as well. His mother had always claimed it calmed her down. It had been her favorite room in the evenings when she did her sewing.

In the midst of this stood a woman dressed in a dark-blue dress, not quite contrasting with her surroundings. Catharijn was a beautiful woman; an oval face with large blue eyes and full lips. Those eyes always made Willem feel like she saw more than anyone wanted to reveal. A few blond curls had escaped her silver-stitched cap in the wind outside, and her cheeks were red from the cold.

Willem smiled at his fiancée and bade her to sit down.

"Catharijn, I didn't expect to see you. Surely it is too cold outside. You should have sent for me instead."

"I apologize, Willem," she said as she laid her elegant hands on her lap. "I received news today that you had returned to Amsterdam."

"No apologies needed," he waved it off. "I trust your family is in good health?"

She nodded and stared at the dark polished wood of the table a moment.

"They are, thank you."

Catharijn's father was a successful merchant who dealt with several businesses, though his main trade was in dye. He was a natural partner for Pieter de Meer. Van Heuvel was not as well off as the De Meers, or as well off as they had been. Willem had to remind himself of that. But the intended marriage was deemed beneficial to both families, especially in terms of connections.

Willem was about to inquire further when Catharijn beat him to it.

"I have come here today... to ask a great favor of you."

"Of course, anything."

"You should not grant it before hearing it. It is a difficult request."

"Is everything all right?" He could easily see the unease on her lovely face. Lips slightly pressed together, brows furrowed as she thought about how to best present her case.

"I have come here to ask you to... "

"Yes?"

She inhaled and then nodded to herself.

"Willem. I have accepted my engagements with no question. But I think I will regret this until my dying day if I don't ask this favor of you."

Willem smiled.

"You must ask it then, Catharijn, for I still don't know what it is that you have to say."

"All right. I am asking if you will help me break our engagement."

Willem sat back in his chair at this as he took her in. She was serious, no doubt about that. As he searched his own mind, he realized that he was not particularly shocked. Nor upset. He had never truly seen her as his future wife, had he?

"Why now?" he asked, and something in his calm voice visibly relaxed her. She had probably expected a more heated response.

"I... have other prospects," she blushed a little at that, and he forced himself not to smile. "I accepted Geert's proposal. I knew my father wanted that. But he has my brothers to help advance his business. And then when Geert... you know." Willem nodded and looked down a moment. "After that, I was simply transferred to you. I suspect it was the same for you?"

Willem nodded again and looked at her. He hadn't really been asked either. With Geert gone, he was expected to take over his brother's duties. *All* of them.

"What do you intend to do?" he asked her.

"I intend to marry, but my father might shun me for a while. However... if—"

"The engagement is already broken off?"

She smiled thankfully, and continued, "then he will perhaps only be half as mad at me."

"And your mother?"

"She won't have to choose sides. At least after a little while."

Willem nodded thoughtfully. From what little he had seen of the Van Heuvels, he knew the bond between mother and daughter was strong. They always stuck together in social gatherings, whispering and laughing together.

"All right," he said after a little while.

"Really?"

"Mm-hmm. I have no more reason to go through with this than you." In all honesty, he didn't think deceiving her father with their near ruin would be a good foundation for a marriage either. Besides, he had enough of Geert's responsibilities to tend to. If this one wanted out, who was he to say otherwise? "I will talk to Father about it. I am sure he will see reason."

"Thank you, Willem. You have no idea what this means to me." She arose from her chair and he hurried to do the same before following her to the door.

"Shouldn't I take you home, Catharijn?" he asked, looking through a small window by the door, only to see the darkness of winter out there.

"I'll be fine," she said with confidence as he put her fur-trimmed cloak on, the hood resting over her curls. "For what it's worth," she added as he opened the door for her, "I think you will make a good husband for someone one day." And then she disappeared into the cold night of Amsterdam, embraced by the noise of those burghers who went about their business in the dark.

4

Willem opened the door to his father's study with
reverence. As children, he and Geert had been told to stay
out of there. It had been, and still was his father's kingdom,
and only he decided what went on in there. Even their
mother had not entered uninvited.

But things had changed; had they not? Willem stood
with his hand on the handle a moment, squinting a little to
see inside the darkened room. Only glowing embers from
earlier in the day gave off any kind of light. According to
Hendrika, Willem's father was not at home most days now.
He suspected the man was out trying desperately to
manage things with the banks, employees, with his ears out
for a helpful deal. Anything that could save them, prefer-
ably without the rumor of their demise beginning to travel
through the city.

Willem pulled himself together. He only needed something to write with and on, so he headed for his father's
large desk and found some paper and a pencil. He brought
it back to the parlor and wrote the letters he needed to. To
his landlady in Leiden, asking to have his things sent back
to Amsterdam; to friends he would not be returning to.

After that, he instructed Hendrika to send them the next day, before he found his thick cloak and fur-trimmed boots and gloves. It was still early night and he would begin his journey to Van Baas to collect the bulb as per his father's instructions. He would find lodgings on his way, show up at Van Baas' in the forenoon, and return to his father later the next night. The sooner he could sell the thing and double his investment, they would be set. *Double?* Willem thought as the frozen ground crunched under his boots. *Triple, quadruple?* Sometimes the prizes for the tulip bulbs were sky high. If they kept their nerve, they could be saved by this little flower, one that he hadn't even heard of before. He had heard of Van Baas, of course, and that eased his worries somewhat. He also trusted his father, so hopefully, this would be their solution. Pieter de Meer was after all an unstoppable force when it came to making deals. *Yes,* Willem thought as he hefted his cloak better around him in the freezing cold, *Keep nature out of this, and it will work. It has to.*

As he walked along the Prinsengracht, he noticed the thin sheet of ice in the canal and wished for the warming winds of spring. As it was now, his cheeks burned from the cold; and he was out to buy a tulip. He shook his head at the insanity. He knew the cultivators grew their treasures inside under glass as well as in the dirt in their gardens. It still struck him as idiotic to buy something that would not even grow before spring. And even then, the flowers would only show the world their beauty for a mere week.

Willem kept on. People would usually still be outside at this hour, but the cold left him alone now and then. The other people he saw were huddled in their warm clothing as well. He thought briefly of his conversation with Catharijn but found it preoccupied him less than he expected it should. She was beautiful and from a good family, but he also found, like her, that it mattered little now. Geert had gotten along with her much better, as he had taken some time to get to know her after their engagement. Willem had taken the first chance he got after Geert's death to go back to Leiden and pretend nothing had changed. But even there, where he had gotten used to being without his brother as Geert had left the university a year prior, things were not the same anymore. And now he was walking through the streets at home, searching for a tulip, *a winter tulip*, he thought. He gave a lopsided smile under his hood as someone bumped into him, pushing him towards the brick wall of a nearby house.

"Hey!" he exclaimed as he got his bearing and saw the figure of a woman running away from him. A gray cloak covered her, but it didn't hide the lower part of her skirts as she ran down the street ahead of him. His first instinct was to check for his purse, but the money was all there. Then he noticed the woman looking behind her as her running slowed somewhat, though she kept going.

"Do you need help?" he half shouted after her, not wishing to draw the attention of anyone who might be looking for her. She seemed scared and in a hurry, proven by how she flew around a corner further ahead. Willem sped up to see where she had gone but came upon the Lauriergracht and no woman. Or anyone else, for that matter. She must have taken a side street somewhere.

Willem shrugged but didn't really feel that lightly about it. Still, there was little he could do to help if she were not there. He walked on by the canal, figuring it would lead him in the right direction anyway. He was headed north-east to find Van Baas and had to cross the streets of Jordaan either way.

He did, however, not get far, before he witnessed something strange again. There was a sharp voice behind him, a little high pitched. He expected to see a child before he turned and confirmed it. Two figures had entered the street behind him, a man and a boy that caught up to him, shouting at him.

"Leave my sister alone!"

The man didn't respond to this with anything but a backhanded slap that sent the boy reeling to the ground. He could not be more than ten, Willem judged in the weak light and distance between them.

"You bastard!" the boy shouted, not willing to give up despite his meager odds against a grown man. "Stay away from my sister, you miserable piece of shit."

"Shut your mouth, you little bastard," the man wheezed back at him, angered enough now to break his steps and go back to the boy.

No, this won't do, Willem thought as he began walking back towards them. He hadn't been in many fights in his life, and the few he had been in were, for the most part, drunken scuffles in Leiden. But this blatant beating of a child did not sit well with him. He could at least give the boy enough room to leave.

But he never got close enough.

As the man went back for the boy who stood his ground, something that should not be possible happened. Willem froze in his steps as he saw the boy, fists clenched at his sides, begin to glow. It was like a fire had been lit within him, beginning in his chest and spreading all throughout his body. It wasn't a light that lit up the street, no, it was a warm golden-red glow.

Willem stared in utter disbelief at the sight, but the man did not. He was quick to react and grab the boy's arm, yanking him towards him so he lost his balance.

"Oh, no you don't, you misbegotten bastard. You listen to me," he growled and bent down, his face inches from the boy's. "*You* will stay away from your sister. In fact, you'll do so by turning around and walking into the canal."

"Yes I will," the boy said as the reddish glow faded. The

man let go of him and headed out of the street, back the way he had likely come, the way Willem had come, without turning back to see what the boy did.

But Willem saw. He stared in shock as the boy straightened, reddish glow draining from him, and turned toward the canal. Then he simply walked straight towards it. The low wall hindered him a mere moment, before the little body tipped over and splashed into the icy water below.

5

"What?" Willem whispered to himself as he realized what had happened. Then his body reacted without him telling it to, and he sprang towards the place where the boy had fallen over the wall. His pulse was hammering in his ears before he reached the low wall. Despite not wanting to, he looked over it and down into the water. It was murky with thin pieces of floating ice where the boy had hit and broken it. The boy screamed as he thrashed around down there, head bobbing under too often. He was not a swimmer.

Willem forgot to breathe. Remembered a choked sound, a face under the water, his arms held behind him. Remembered thrashing wildly to get free to no avail.

Another scream pierced the cold, hard air.

Willem's arms *were* free.

He didn't think. Simply stepped up on the wall. The only thing he had the wherewithal to do before he jumped, was to yank loose the heavy cloak he wore.

The water felt like it punched all of him at once as he landed in it. It was shockingly and painfully cold as it pulled him down, and oh so dark. He couldn't see a thing, yet he managed to reach the surface as the impact of his jump lessened.

He breached the surface with a desperate gasp, more from the biting cold than any long-term lack of air.

"Help!" the boy shouted next to him before his head went under again.

Willem kicked against the water with his legs and grabbed the boy so he could hold his head over the surface, but the boy fought him in his panic. With the cold, it was hard to keep hold of him despite their differences in size.

"You need to calm down!" Willem shouted as he lost hold of him a moment, and he went under again. Willem ducked under, almost screaming against the biting pain on his face as he got hold of the boy and managed to get both of them above the surface.

"Calm down or you'll go under again!" Willem shouted. Somehow, in his panic, the boy seemed to listen, because he stopped fighting, though he did not go completely limp.

"Oh, God!" Willem exclaimed as he now had the time to look around. There was water on all sides, except behind them where they'd come from. There was only the wall there, high and slimy from the grimy water of the canal.

"Help!" he shouted, panic threatening to overcome him as well now as he remembered the empty street. The people in the houses might hesitate to come outside if they thought something violent was going on out there. They didn't have time for hesitation. Willem could feel his muscles stiffening, his movements slowing down. He was a good swimmer, having learned one lazy summer in his childhood when the family had stayed in the house in Haarlem. But swimming was not the issue now. They would drown because the freezing cold was claiming all his strength.

He kept shouting for help; the boy as well, though his voice grew weaker too fast. Willem struggled to keep them both afloat, but wouldn't let go of the boy. Instead, he kept him up as his own head began to bob under the surface, making him spit the foul-tasting water between his shouts.

"Claes?" A piercing shout that turned into a scream came from above, as the owner of the voice realized that said Claes was indeed in the water.

"Lia, help!" the boy, Claes, shouted.

"Hang on!" she shouted as Willem managed to look up without his head going under. It was a dark-haired woman, gray cloak over her hair, which hung loose like curtains framing her lovely face as she glanced around. The woman from earlier, he managed to think through his strained treading of the water.

"Grab on to this!" she shouted as she threw something over the wall. Something dark. It took a moment longer for Willem to realize it was his own cloak, and then another trip under the surface before he saw that she was using it as she would a rope.

"Grab on!" the woman shouted as the cloak came near enough for them to do so. It required a jump from Willem's side and the woman hanging with her upper body over the wall, for him to reach. He managed by kicking against the slick wall under the surface. He saw, with a weakened sense of triumph, that Claes was able to grab hold of the end of it, before Willem sank back into the canal's cold embrace. At least the boy would make it.

"What are you doing?" the woman screamed at him, her face full of anger. So strange. He had thought her so beautiful a moment ago. Thinking became harder as the pain of the cold overpowered him.

"You can't lift us both," he managed to get out through his chattering teeth. There was not enough voice in him for her to hear him, but the boy did.

"Get up here, and grab hold, Mynheer," he said. His young face was strained from the pain and cold, his teeth visibly chattering as well. His dark hair lay plastered to his forehead and his clothes clung to him. Only his lower legs were still under the water. "Grab hold," Claes repeated, his face serious despite the fear he must have felt. Willem didn't know why, but he found that he swam closer to the wall again and did as told. It was madness, a part of his brain screamed at him. The woman couldn't pull them up. Willem was sure she couldn't pull the boy up on his own either. He kicked against the wall and, with a strength he didn't know from where it came, he shot out of the icy water and grabbed onto the cloak with enough of a grip not to fall back down again.

"Hold on, Mynheer," Claes said, his body shivering so hard his voice came out all shaky now. Willem managed to brace his legs against the wall, just like the boy. It was a relief to be out of the heavy pull of the water, but the cold winter air did nothing to appease his freezing and protesting body.

He felt a tug upward on the cloak and wondered how long the woman would be able to hold on before someone came by or they both fell back into the canal. He could focus on little but holding on, his shivering hands threatening to make him lose his grip.

A faint light came from above and Willem felt a flutter of hope that someone had come to aid them, but as he glanced up he saw that was not the case. It was the woman. The same reddish glow he had seen in the boy now emanated from her as she pulled at the cloak. She pulled both of them up along the slippery wall in a slow and steady motion. Willem stared up at her, enthralled in her glowing form, her face frozen in concentration as she worked to save them. Her eyes shone a deep red, unlike the rest of her. Under any other circumstances, he would have thought her a demon, but now the beauty of it, the hope, made him think they were the eyes of an angel.

She gave a strained gasp as Willem and the boy reached the top, where she grabbed the back of both their shirts to help drag them over the wall. Willem collided with the hard and unyielding frozen ground, while one of his legs remained sprawled up against the wall. The warm and reddish light faded, the golden rays with it. Voices came closer — and then came the blissful warm calm that, in the end, always shrouded those freezing to death.

6

"He's been slipping in and out of consciousness," a female voice said. It was strange to him, yet somehow Willem felt he'd heard it before. Then his attention, such as it was, was diverted elsewhere as he felt himself lowered onto a bed. It was not a feathered bed with springs to softly receive him, but a straw-filled mattress, that softened the blunt landing on his back. He felt the air leave his lungs and then blacked out again.

The next time he came to, confusion had not left him. There was an ache in his chest he vaguely wondered about, until his throat exploded into a coughing fit he could not brace himself against.

"Cornelia," an authoritative female voice said. "We need water. Heat it, and add these."

"Yes, Oma," she said.

"And make sure it's enough for both of them."

"Who is this man?" a male voice asked.

"No idea," the woman referred to as grandmother said. "But without him, Claes would be dead, so let's repay him with preventing his death."

Willem heard some rustling with fabric; soft and swift

footfalls on the floor nearby. He had a sense there were many people nearby, scurrying about. He could hear strong coughing nearby as well. The boy? Claes. Willem hoped he had made it.

He felt himself drift away again, but his shivering body refused to let him rest. He could hardly manage to open his eyes, he wanted nothing more than sleep, but the incessant people around kept talking and moving about.

"All right. Off with their clothes."

"No..." Willem tried protesting.

"This is not the time to be shy, young man," the same order-giving woman said. "Your clothes are like ice. We need to warm you up."

Willem could feel the sopping wet clothes stripped from his body as he lay motionless except for the incessant shivering. Saw people above him like shadows as they moved methodically, lifting and rolling him when needed to get the garments off.

It didn't help, he thought. He was still freezing, and now he was naked too.

"And you, Fransiska, I need these blankets heated. Not so they burn the skin but keep them near the oven. Get Marien and the children to help you. All the blankets we can muster."

"Yes, Alice," a low spoken woman said.

Alice? Willem managed to think as someone rubbed a blanket over him. He was not aware enough to be ashamed now. Was the Oma called Alice? Come to think of it, she did speak a little differently.

He tried opening his eyes but saw only a wooden wall around his head, and then passed out again as a coughing fit threatened to overpower him. Whether it did or not, he was blissfully unaware.

Someone else's coughing pulled him back. The boy again. Willem could still see him thrashing in the water. He couldn't swim. He saw him go under. Willem groaned at the memory.

"Andries," the authoritative voice of Alice sounded through the room. "This man needs some clothes. I have Marien wringing his own out, but they won't be dry in hours yet."

"I have some spare," the man answered.

"Good. We need to cover him up and keep him warm. I've found new ones for Claes."

Shortly after, Willem felt himself moved and shifted again as dry clothes were now pulled on him. A shirt and breeches, he guessed. They smelled faintly of tobacco and soap and did nothing to help warm his body. He tried sitting up but was pushed back onto the mattress.

"Here," a female voice said before the strong smell of ginger reached him. He thought it was the voice he recognized. "You need to drink," the voice urged. Its owner helped Willem raise his head enough to drink from a cup of warm... tea? He had no idea. It tasted awful, and he began coughing again. The taste of ginger might be the strongest, but he did not appreciate the blend with nutmeg and whatever else foul-tasting things were in there.

"What...?" he croaked.

"It's Oma's concoction," the voice said. "Just drink. It will help with your coughing."

Willem tried opening his eyes, feeling like a newborn kitten struggling to do so. But he managed and looked right into the blurry, yet unmistakable face of the woman who had turned into red gold and saved him and the boy.

"You need to drink," she urged him. "Trust me. Oma knows best."

In his shock-ridden mind, he found that he did trust her. How could he not? He might have jumped in after the boy, but she had saved them both. He wasn't quite sure how, but he knew it to be true. So, he drank. Gulped down the strong-tasting liquid, drops spilling over the rim and running down his cheek. The warm spill felt like torture against his shivering and freezing skin.

"Marien, how are you coming along?" Alice shouted from somewhere else while murmuring sweet words to someone. It had to be young Claes. Willem could hear a pause in his coughing, so he thought he must be getting the same brew.

"Right here, Alice," the voice of Marien came. Willem could see nothing with the wooden walls all around him, an alcove maybe? It didn't matter and moments later, heated blankets were laid on top of him and around him. The sensation felt like a relief first before he realized it did not stop him from keeping on freezing.

"How long were they in the canal?"

"Not long, I think. I was trying to get away from Cec. I think Claes might have followed me."

"Cec? Again?"

The woman withdrew from Willem, talking to someone he couldn't see.

"Yes."

"Where's Andries?"

"Don't bother him with that now," the woman insisted. "They can't have been in the water more than a few minutes."

"That's more than enough for freezing to death this time of year," Alice said.

A few minutes at the most, Willem wanted to say but found he had no voice. He couldn't get the taste of ginger root out of his mouth either.

"If this man hadn't been there, Claes would have drowned," the woman said. "You know how afraid he is of water."

"I do," Alice said, "which makes me wonder." She left it hanging there. Willem was certain there was something to

34

both the women's words, but couldn't gather his wits to think. Instead, he lay shaking under the blankets.

"All right," Alice said, sounding like she'd come to a decision. "There's nothing to be done about it now I suppose, and I don't want Andries ending up in the canal either."

The woman gave a snort at that. "God knows he's done that enough."

"Yes, but there's a difference when it's the cold of winter. Anyway — enough of this. We'll deal with it when we're sure these two are over the worst."

"Yes," the woman agreed. There was a pause, and then; "he saw me."

Another pause.

"You had no choice, child. It was that or let your brother die."

"I know, but he is not affiliated with us. I'm sure of it. There was too much surprise in him at the sight of me."

Alice let out a deep sigh wherever she stood, hidden from Willem's half-focused view.

"We'll deal with it. For now, you're to make sure he doesn't freeze to death."

"But—"

"I'll tend to Claes. He's younger, weaker. No arguing now, Cornelia."

"Yes, Oma."

Willem heard the rustling of the woman's, Cornelia's skirts, as she got up. He felt the blankets on the other end of the bed be tucked more closely around his bare feet before she lifted them near his upper body. The little shift in temperature was enough to make him groan in pain as his teeth chattered uncontrollably. Cornelia quickly kicked her shoes off before she gathered her skirts and got in under the blankets with him. The shock of this startled him despite everything else.

"It's all right," she said as she snuggled into him, placing her arm around him, cradling his head with the other, his face nuzzled against her neck. "I'll keep you warm."

For the first time since being thrown on the mattress, his eyes managed to open fully, not that he saw much more than before. He was indeed in an alcove. Other than that, he saw little more than the curve of Cornelia's neck and her flowing dark hair on the pillow they shared, a hint of copper in it. Auburn? It was hard to tell without proper lighting. She did indeed feel warm against his shivering frame, firm and curvy as well.

"I don't... " he began, his voice weak. "I don't think your family will approve of this," he tried.

"Well," she said, her voice low, almost a whisper; friendly, warm. "It's me or Andries, and he doesn't want to." Willem could feel a slight tremor in her body as she laughed softly, even through his own shaking. "You need to keep warm," she continued. "Body heat helps with that. My name's Cornelia by the way, but you can call me Lia."

"Willem," he croaked. "Wim."

"All right, Wim. You try and get some sleep. I'll call Oma if you need her."

Somehow, Willem felt he didn't need any oma at the moment. Nor did he think he could get any sleep the way he shivered and while his chest ached. Still, the strong brew he had been given had at least staved off his cough. He heard the boy further off in the house somewhere. He still coughed now and then, but at least he got some respite between the attacks. The house quieted as well. There were fewer footsteps and fewer voices murmuring. Willem had no idea what time it was and didn't have the wherewithal to think about it, nor did he question where he was or who these people were. Instead, he fell asleep while shivering and exhausted in a strange woman's arms.

He awoke a while later, still feeling icy cold, but calm

and more aware. His fingers and toes didn't hurt anymore, and his teeth were not knocking uncontrollably against each other. He was again shocked to find Cornelia in the bed. She lay closely entwined with him, and he realized his arms were now around her as well. He must have done that in his sleep. She smelled of soap and ginger. He found he didn't mind that like he minded the taste in the brew from earlier. The house was quiet now and the lights had been snuffed out. Only a faint glow allowed him to see any contours, probably embers from a dying fire somewhere.

"Are you all right?" he heard Cornelia say, close to his ear. She must have sensed him being awake. "You're as cold as ice." A soft hand stroked his cheek and neck, a pleasant gesture that made him close his eyes. He didn't open them again. Simply drifted off to sleep, exhausted, yet safe and comfortable with no care for where he was.

❧ 7 ❧

The next time Willem awoke, it was still dark, but distant noises told him the city was beginning to wake up out there. At least, he thought it was the city. He could be in Constantinople for all he knew. How long had he been out? He could feel his pulse quickening at the thought of what might have been going on while he was out of it.

"You're still in Amsterdam," Cornelia said next to him, close to him.

Willem was immediately drawn back to the alcove, the events of the previous night returned to him. As much as he had understood of them at the time. He could feel her fingers stroking his hair in a calm rhythm. His pulse slowed, and he relaxed. He was not freezing anymore, nor was his skin cold. Why was she still there? He didn't mind. It felt oddly comforting and intimate, though he knew it wasn't seemly. He had never spent a whole night in bed with a woman before, not like this. There had been the shortsighted and short-time affair with a merchant's daughter back in Leiden. It had involved different activities that required sneaking into the house after everyone had turned in for the night, and sneaking out again before daylight. None of that had involved this kind of intimacy. Of course, he'd been exposed to freezing water in the winter, so he supposed normal rules were put aside to keep him warm. That was it after all. He could feel Cornelia's long skirts and bodice under the blankets. He had no idea how he'd dared put his arms around her during the night, but now he didn't want to let go.

"Where in Amsterdam?" he asked her after a little while, wondering whether she had slept at all or only watched him to make sure he was all right.

"Rozenstraat. You're in our home. You're safe here."

Not far from his father's home then. Willem certainly hadn't gotten far last night.

"What happened at the canal?" he asked. He remembered everything up until being pulled out of the canal, but it had flown by so fast.

"You don't remember?"

Did he sense a certain hope in her at that? Relief?

"No, I remember, but I don't understand most of it."

She kept stroking his hair, such a satisfying sensation that lulled him into a pleasant calm. "Tell me what happened before I got there, please."

He did. Went with the truth of it all. Knew she wouldn't call him insane. Remembered her talking to her grandmother about it the night before.

"The boy simply turned around and walked into the canal. Walked, I tell you. No jumping. Walked straight into the low wall and then toppled over when his feet stopped and the rest of him moved forward."

He felt her other arm hold him a little tighter at that, concern still for what had happened to her brother, he supposed.

"What happened?" he pressed. "One thing is a man telling a boy to jump into a canal. That is bad enough, but it actually working? And how did you pull us out of the water? There was no one else but you there."

"I'm sorry, Wim. You saw a lot you weren't supposed to yesterday."

"Well?"

She sighed, the movement of it pushing against him.

"It is our... gifts," she began, sounding like she didn't quite like that word. "We are able to do things others can't."

"Like telling a poor boy to wander into a freezing canal?" Willem couldn't hide the disdain in his voice.

"Like that. There are those that care more for their own pride and wants among us, as it is with you."

There was no arguing that.

"How did you pull us out?" he repeated.

"Claes and I... we can... let's just say we are very strong when we need to be."

"You lifted us out of the water... " Willem's words came out slow and not as a question. He'd seen it; had he not? He remembered it in flashes. This glow of red light emanating from her as she pulled them up, Willem's cloak thankfully holding at the seams.

"I did. I had to get you out."

"Yes. Thank you."

He heard her give a soft scoff, like there was a smile there.

"No. Thank *you*, Wim. I didn't know Claes had followed me. He's not as strong as me yet, but he wants to protect me. Without your quick thinking... he would be dead now." Her voice broke a little at the thought and her hand stopped stroking his hair. Willem shifted his position a little. He had been lying still, not wanting her to leave, but now he moved his hand to the side of her face. He gently stroked her soft hair away from her face before resting it there. She didn't seem to mind.

"My quick thinking, as you call it, would only have staved off the inevitable. Without you, well... "

They lay in silence a moment. Somewhere in the building, a door opened and closed, but no one stirred near them.

"Who was that man?" Willem finally asked.

"Cec. He's been after me a while now. Found out about my ability, and... "

"And what?" Willem had suspected the man had dishonorable thoughts regarding her but was not so certain now. At least when it came to what kind of dishonorable thoughts.

"He's a thief. Breaks into wealthy homes, but his control doesn't last all that long. He's weak in that respect, thankfully. But if he keeps it up long enough... "

"You mean he plans to make use of you for thieving?"

Cornelia moved a little, indicating a shrug at this. "I would be excellent at opening a safe; don't you think?"

"I take it you refused him?"

"Yes. He might be fine with stealing from others and controlling them, but I'm not. I have other plans."

"With regards to stealing?"

"No," she laughed softly at that. "With regards to dressmaking. That's what I want to be. A dressmaker. One of the best."

"A more reputable profession than a safe breaker I'm sure."

"Exactly."

She would need to work hard to gain a good reputation for that, especially if she wanted the richer women in town as customers. Somehow, Willem didn't think she lacked the will to do it.

Coughing broke the silence of the house and they soon heard a soothing, soft voice trying to comfort young Claes.

"I'm so happy he's alive," Cornelia said, her fingers

starting their pleasant journey back and forth through his hair again. "But what on God's earth compelled you to jump after him at this time of year?"

Willem tensed.

"I... my brother died less than a year ago. Almost the same way." Willem found he had trouble getting the words out. Felt Cornelia's arms tighten around him for comfort. She had felt the fear of losing a brother after all. "He didn't freeze to death, but... "

"It's all right. You don't have to think about that now."

He never wanted to think about it. And yet the thoughts came sneaking up on him when he least expected it. He couldn't even look at the Oude Kerk without having every memory flung in his face. When in the city, he always made an effort not to pass by that particular building.

Soft footfalls went by the alcove, reminding them that the world would soon return to normal. There were more voices to be heard outside as well; people shouting messages or prices of their wares, others greeting each other in the early hours. The fire was rekindled at some point as the familiar crackle could be heard as well as the soft smell of smoke and burning firewood. With all this came light, and Willem could now see Cornelia's face again. Youthful and striking —she could be no more than twenty. She had a soft smile on her lips that at the least told him she was not unhappy at having shared the alcove with him. Even if he'd been half frozen to death most of the time.

A young red-headed boy wandered into view, carrying an earthenware jug in his hand. He glanced shyly at them where they lay under the blankets, curious about the stranger in the house. Cornelia noticed him after Willem and turned her head to see clearly as the jug in the boy's little hand shifted form. Willem gasped as it moved in the air, though still on the boy's flat hand. It melted and reassembled as a perfectly round lump of clay, before it shifted back to its original form.

Willem stared. Stunned and disbelieving, despite everything that had happened.

"Lieve, stop that," Cornelia told the child. "Go help your mother."

Lieve got a sour look on his face at the chiding but did as told nonetheless.

"I'm sorry," Cornelia said. "The little ones are curious and not good at hiding what should stay hidden."

"He... " Willem said, still in shock at what the boy had done. "That was like magic——"

"Oh no." Cornelia laughed that off. "That doesn't——"

"How are we feeling this morning?" a familiar voice broke in. A tall and stately woman came into view in the alcove's opening, looking down at them with a friendly smile. She had voluminous almost white hair. It wasn't gray. It had a distinct reddish-golden tint to it, like it had once been red before slowly fading as she grew older. This had to be Alice.

"He stopped shaking during the night, but was cold to the touch for a long time," Cornelia told her grandmother. "Now he seems much improved."

"No doubt the company helped," Alice said with a lopsided smile that made Willem blush. She didn't seem reproachful at this unusual bed arrangement though. It had, after all, been her idea. "How's the chest then?"

"What?" Willem managed in his embarrassed confusion. He knew they couldn't stay this way any longer now, and yet they both still held on to each other under the layers of blankets.

"The chest...?" she gave him a look, as she didn't yet know his name.

"Willem," he said. "And it's fine?"

"Good to hear you sounding so sure. I've got breakfast

on. I'll have a look at you after." And then she disappeared from view. Willem could feel a pressure in his chest, and a difficulty in taking deep breaths, but he felt alert and warm. Surely he was fine.

A door opened nearby; the sound of the outside amplified a moment before it closed again. Willem didn't pay it much heed as he remained in Cornelia's arms for the remaining few moments that he still could. Another person stepped into view from their alcove, actually pausing to peek inside. Willem turned to see a man this time, medium height with an almost lanky body that looked like it was due to little food more than anything. The smell of old alcohol that accompanied him indicated he had traded the need for sustenance with the need for strong drink. It was a tired face that gazed at them, angular and with an uneven nose that had once been broken. A graying beard covered the lower part of the face but couldn't hide a white scar that ran from his left temple and just over his cheekbone. It was the eyes that struck Willem though. Large blue eyes that were almost shielded by the unruly shoulder-length hair around the man's scraggly face. But not the eyes, no they were alert and knowing, like they laughed at the world no matter what the soul behind them said.

"I heard about the visitor," he said in a surprisingly ordinary voice. Willem didn't know why he had expected anything else. "I see you didn't waste any time, Lia." He snickered at his own comment, like it was a joke.

"Never you mind," she snapped back, not afraid of him, but not fond of him either. That much was clear from the way she sat up at the sight of him. She had not done that with the others. "Oma's got food on the stove. Go there and mind your own business."

The man looked at her a moment before walking off, snickering on his way.

"Friend of yours?" Willem asked, thinking that at least

he was not likely to be her husband. Probably not her father either, the way he'd made fun of them instead of being angered.

"That's just Yorov," Cornelia said and drew the blankets to the side. "Don't mind him. He's of no importance." She inched over to the side of the bed and got out. A shiver of cold ran through Willem, but it had nothing to do with the actual warmth of her body disappearing from his side. It was the realization that the strange and unusual night was now over.

8

The day after Willem's jump into a freezing canal turned
out to be a sunny one after the morning's fog lifted. After
breakfast, Willem had been told to rest out back in the
garden, a courtyard placed away from the out-facing facade
of what he deemed to be Alice's house. She was adamant
that the fresh air was good for Willem's and Claes' coughs,
but had ordered them into several blankets first. And so,
Willem found himself in what was a part of a large courtyard behind the house. Sections of it had been walled in,
sequestered off from the neighbors. All except the resi-
dents of one house, but they all seemed to move freely
between their homes, working and talking together all the
time, sharing meals and gossip.

Willem's cough had returned during breakfast, making
it impossible for him to eat more than half a bowl of
porridge. He couldn't quite decide what was worse, as he
wasn't fond of porridge. Not used to it either. He had
awoken to a different world as he had been invited to the
table; a table surrounded by what he surmised to be two
families at the least. Men, women, and children, though he
was not sure of their relationships yet. There were no

servants in the house, and no discernible hierarchy to be seen, except for the fact that the head of the table was Alice's place. That made sense to him. She was the matriarch of the house, no doubt about that, and they all listened to her, even the men. No questioning her orders if she gave them.

Which she did now as well, as she joined Willem and Claes with two cups in her hands. Whatever was in them was hot, the white steam rising in the cold air. Willem smelled the ginger and various spices before the cup was proffered.

"You need to drink. You know it worked well last night," Alice insisted. He had learned a few things so far. Her late husband's family name was Aarden, but she herself had been married off at a young age from Ireland. Which was why she spoke with an accent. She was also right about her disgusting brew, it did soothe his chest and throat, so he took it and forced the liquid down.

"Good," she said with a smile. "There's a nice dollop of brandy in there too. It helps with the pain."

Willem could taste a lot of things in the brew, and from what he gathered, none of it blended well together.

"Alice," a male voice closer to the house said. They all looked up to see the man Andries, a fair-haired and handsome man that also seemed to wield some authority in the households. He sure had their respect. "Lia and I are done," he said as the two women called Fransiska and Marien came out the door behind him. Their glances at the muscular man told Willem that they at least were not related.

Andries nodded towards Claes.

"All right if I have a word with him now?"

Claes, who had emptied his cup gave a contented sigh at having finished drinking as well as a grimace at the taste.

"Might be best for him to go inside now anyway," Alice

said as she looked at the boy. Unlike Willem, Claes was more affected by the fall into the water the previous night. His cough was worse, and his pale skin not quite willing to get its luster back. Still, Alice didn't seem overly worried, so Willem hoped time would restore the boy. Alice helped Claes to his feet and he shuffled towards Andries who took him inside.

"I'm grateful for all your help, Mrs. Aarden," Willem began as he lowered the empty cup. "But I had business for my father yesterday when I came over your grandson. I must return home."

Alice nodded. "You're free to do as you like, of course, but I've a mind to look you over for another day. You did me a grand favor yesterday, one I can't ever repay, so it's the least I can do."

"Why? Is something wrong?"

"The ache in your chest. We want them lungs to be healthy and strong, don't we?"

Willem noticed Cornelia stepping through the back door, her long and loose hair, truly auburn in the strong sun. Maybe he could stay another day? What would it hurt anyway? He had lost the contract yesterday. What was one more day in a house where people welcomed you in and shared what little they had, when the alternative was going home to his father to admit the valuable contract was lost?

Alice called for the red-headed boy when Willem agreed to her suggestion. She stated he could deliver a message to Willem's father, so they would not worry when he didn't return home after his intended journey. As Cornelia sat down beside him in the sunlight, he scribbled down a message on the piece of paper that Alice provided and handed it to the boy. At once the paper shifted and divided into several small pieces that hovered above the child's hand.

"Lieve," Alice reproached him. "Not out here where the neighbors can see you."

"Nobody can see over the fences," the boy protested, making Alice shake her head in consternation.

"Lieve?" another voice shouted from the other house before the woman, Fransiska stuck her head out the door. "Are you bothering Mrs. Aarden?"

"No, Mama."

"He's only doing me a favor," Alice chimed in and Fransiska nodded and ducked inside again. A smaller boy came running out the same door, the same red hair as Lieve, but he was no more than four years old, Willem guessed.

"You run along now," Alice told Lieve, urging him on as she turned and lifted up the smaller boy as he reached her.

"It's cold," he wailed.

"Then why did you come outside, child?" Alice said and headed for the other house. "Let's find your mother."

"Lieve's brother?" Willem asked Cornelia, aware of her closeness, yet also the fact that he could not touch her now.

"Cousin," she said as she watched her grandmother disappear into the other house with the little boy. "That's Eadmund. He's named for Oma's father.

"Who's the mother then?"

"Marien. She and Fransiska each had children by two red-headed cousins. I guess they have the same taste in men," she smirked. Willem couldn't help smiling with her, though it seemed strange to him to choose a spouse based on appearance. After all, that had nothing to do with his own engagement, which he now realized he was becoming more thrilled to ask his father to break.

"I found this in your cloak," Cornelia said and handed him his purse and a small letter. The shift in the conversation distracted him enough that it took a moment for him to realize that she had just handed him his father's contract. He drew breath and then began coughing, all the while staring at the sealed envelope. He had not caused his father's certain ruin by saving a drowning child. The relief flooded him so hard he became aware that he had pushed the thought from his mind the whole time. Especially during the night.

He glanced at Cornelia who sat with a fur-trimmed coat around her, light gray in color. He had noticed that the Aarden's, and whoever lived in the other house, had simple clothes, no expensive colors, but they were all of good quality. Someone in the household knew how to wield a needle, and judging by last night's conversation, he suspected whom. To think of all the fabrics he, of all people, could have given her only a few months ago.

"Thank you," he said as he realized he hadn't said a word since the contract had landed in his hand.

"Keep that purse out of Yorov's sight," Cornelia warned, not understanding which of the objects had the true value.

"Who is he anyway?" Willem asked, doing as told and stuffing his valuables under all the blankets. They honestly did the trick, keeping him warm, while he enjoyed the fresh air. The flower beds around them were barren and the only smell in the courtyard came from a neighbor who was frying onions. That smell alone made Willem's mouth water.

Cornelia shrugged, and then hugged her arms tight around her. He's just... Yorov. He's Marien and Fransiska's father, but let me make it clear. He lives with them. Not the other way around."

Somehow, remembering the strong smell of alcohol, Willem could believe that. "I've never heard a name like that before."

"Well, it's... I don't really know what it is. He's been here since I was a girl. I guess I never questioned it."

"First name or last?"

"Don't know. He's just... Yorov."

"And he has a... gift, as you called it as well?"

She smiled weakly then and he noticed she was shivering. He wanted nothing more than to share his blankets with her, but that was not possible anymore.

"Most of us have some sort of ability. Not all, but most. Some are born without them."

"Alice?"

"It's not really my place to say... but she won't mind I guess. She can tell what people around her feel. Sometimes, I wish I had inherited her ability," Cornelia said and gave him a warm smile before getting up. She needed to go inside for a while, as it was too cold for her to sit still with only a coat. As she walked away, Willem was struck by all the things he wanted to know about her. Had she been born here? Where were her parents? Why was her dream to become a dressmaker? He could ask her these things later, but it was hard with so many people around all the time. Their little cocoon of spellbound intimacy had broken and would not enclose them again. At least not now. Willem sighed as he realized he was infatuated with this woman who had saved his life, and who he had only known for less than a full day. No, he wanted to know her better, that much was clear. But as if to prove the vibrant, busy and interrupting state of the two houses, Arend came walking out of Alice's house. The thin blond man dipped his chin in Willem's direction as he walked into the other house. Willem had come to understand that he was Andries' brother, but had not yet figured out which house they lived in. From Cornelia's words though, it didn't surprise him a few moments later when the lanky form of Yorov came out from his daughters' house. What did surprise him, was the man's changed direction toward Willem when he noticed him.

"Well, what have we here? Mynheer Wim, himself." It was clear the man had had some more to drink since last night and now reeked of tobacco as well. He slumped down beside Willem and leaned against the fence, sighing in contentment at not having to stay upright anymore. Unlike Alice, who one could tell was a foreigner by her clear accent, there was only a hint of it in this man's speech. It was enough, though, to tell Willem that he wasn't a Dutchman.

"Saw the clothes my girl has been washing out, I did. Fancy garments that. Are you rich, boy?"

Willem had completely forgotten about his own clothes until now, wearing Andries' still, and not caring, covered as he was by layers of warmth.

"No," he answered honestly. "My father is," he added with a little defiance and began coughing. Yorov waited patiently until he stopped. Then he procured a bottle containing unknown spirits from his coat's inner pocket. The man didn't seem to mind the cold so much. *Perhaps the alcohol warms him?* Willem winced at the thought. It had not warmed Geert.

"So, you're one of them heirs then."

Willem supposed he was. But he was not supposed to be, was he?

"I hear you know all about us now," Yorov continued as he took a slow swig from his bottle, enjoying the taste and effect it seemed. Willem shook his head as the man offered him some.

"I know a little," he said instead.

"We're supposed to keep hidden from the likes of you, you know. Lead to nothing but trouble when ordinary folk finds out. It's ridiculous. We should rule those weaker than us, not be frightened by them."

"What kind of trouble?"

Yorov's daughter Fransiska exited the other house and glared at her father as she passed through the courtyard on her way to Alice's. Willem still noticed her eyes darting to the bottle in Yorov's hand with longing. They had one thing in common it seemed. Yorov drank some more, apparently not caring about his offspring's disrespectful glare. He pursed his lips and then nodded sideways a few times, considering Willem's question.

"Aren't we all greedy? I heard you helped Lia out of a bind with young Cec."

Young Cec? He sounded like he knew the man well.

"Isn't that man like you?"

"Yes, but no different than your kind. It's use or be used in this world. Haven't you learned that yet? Eh... maybe you rich folks don't have to think about that." Yorov waved it off and drank some more, before he began rummaging through his pockets, clearly looking for something and not finding it. "Where's my damn pipe?" he said to himself and then gave up. Willem was glad. He didn't think the ever-threatening cough would be better with the smoke.

"I had a small fortune once, you know," Yorov went on, "But it vanished, just like that." He raised his hand to make the point, to snap his fingers, but the small explosion of shimmering pink light from the man's fingers made Willem startle in surprise.

"Hah," Yorov barked. "Not used to it yet, huh?"

"What... what, was that?"

"You don't want to know, boy. Let's just say it hurts. Anyway. My fortune. I had it and it was snatched away from me. No man should feel safe on account of having riches, I'll tell you that, boy. It can fall apart too easily. And then there is no pride, no respect," he spat the last word out, "no name for others to identify your worth. So I ended up here in this misbegotten city." Where he had little respect, Willem was sure, but he realized he was paying attention. The man might be raving on in his drunkenness, but he wasn't wrong, was he? Would Willem's father fall to become like this if the tulip did not save them? Yet again, he was overwhelmed by his grief over his brother's death. Would they even have been in this mess with him still here?

"Oh, they take their pride in it," Yorov said, not noticing the grief on his audience's face. "How they saved the city from the sea, wrestled Mother Nature herself into submission through their little canals. It has given me nothing."

It has given us everything, Willem wanted to say but didn't. Coughs exploded from his chest again, but this time there was no scraping in his throat as he went with it until it ceased. He might have died in one of the canals the night before, but they were a pride to the city; to all of them. To the community of burghers that made the city come alive. It was a different pride than what Yorov longed for. Different from what Willem's father stood to lose.

"Mynheer de Meer," Alice's voice rang out over the enclosed courtyard. He looked up, having not noticed her coming out. "I think your lungs have had enough fresh air for today. Why don't you come inside? I know Lia and Fransiska will have started with the bream. It was caught fresh this morning."

"You're looking lovely as always, Alice," Yorov said, voice level, as Willem managed to get up without losing any of the blankets.

"Never you mind, Yorov," Alice said giving him a look through narrowed eyes.

No, Willem thought as he followed her inside*, that man receives no respect*, nor was Willem certain he was entitled to it. But Willem also realized as the warmth of Alice's busy house welcomed him, that as much as Cornelia drew his attention away from his problems like a lovely and comforting dream, Yorov seemed to have a way of bringing them up inadvertently.

9

Willem was again given use of the alcove, but alone this time. Despite spending a day doing little but talk and eat, he fell asleep in the busy house that smelled of fish for the rest of the night. When he awoke the smell was gone, but a noise denied him returning to his slumber. It was a noise that didn't belong in Alice's house. Willem had not been there long, but he was certain of that much. A door opened, too, with an abrupt motion. It banged into a wall. He heard murmurs from others sleeping nearby, but no one stirred. Willem sat up. He was not covered by a mountain of blankets this night, and they fell off him with ease.

Then he heard it again. A muffled noise. Someone being silenced? He was not sure, and he didn't want to rouse the whole household in case he was mistaken. Still, the feeling of unease overpowered him. He couldn't go back to sleep without having a look at least.

He got out of the alcove and with light steps walked through the house, so different from where he had grown up. No paintings, few decorations, but food, and people's various work strewn about. A different feel to it altogether, even when people slept, you got a sense of life; vibrant and happy.

And so, the muffled whimper Willem heard as he neared the front door in the *voorhuis*, made him certain something was amiss. There stood a candle by the door, for one thing, unattended and shining for no one. So someone had gone to the door in the middle of the night. Who had knocked? And why? An emergency?

A door, a little to the side of the front door stood ajar. Despite being a guest in the house, Willem had no idea what it led to. He soon came to see it was a small room, used for little but storing some fabrics and sewing equipment. Was this Cornelia's workspace?

He never had time to wonder beyond his initial impression, as he came close enough to hear a man's voice. A moment later, he saw him as well. Willem had not gotten a good view of the man in the semidarkness and distance on the Lauriergracht, but he recognized the voice of the man who had ordered young Claes to walk into the canal. And now he saw him as well, young, chestnut-colored hair, his face red with anger as he pushed Cornelia against a table, hand over her mouth. Oddly enough, her eyes looked dull as she stared straight ahead, staring at nothing. It didn't seem like her. She must have been working late in there, the light tipping off Cec. Who else would open the door for him when she was the one closest to it?

"Now you will listen to me and do as I say," the man, Cec, said to her. He removed his hand from her mouth, and Willem saw her nod, slowly and without meaning.

"Yes," she told Cec.

"If you cooperate, we can even retire soon, free from the poor man's stacking debts."

Willem saw Cornelia open her mouth to answer, but then falter as she looked down.

"No," she began, but Cec was quick as he gripped her chin and forced her to look at him.

"I'm not going to lose you this time, Little Bird. We have work to do, remember?"

"Yes," she answered, enthralled by the man again, though with no visible enthusiasm.

"That's right. Please me, and we may even have some fun after," he said as he put his hand on her hip. He slid it up her gray bodice until he grabbed one of her breasts, squeezing and giving her a leering smile she could not react to.

A wave of jealousy hit Willem at the sight, something he had not felt before; anger and indignation at this happening to Cornelia. He didn't think much after that. Didn't stop to consider this man was a threat to everybody he made eye contact with. Instead, Willem turned and grabbed the candlestick. It was made of tin and hefty enough. He moved back towards the little sewing room, and barely had time to blow out the candle before he raised the candlestick and hit it over Cec's head. He heard the man grunt as he went down on one knee, arms going up to cover his head. Willem hit again, this time in the man's unprotected side, as the candle fell to the floor, wax dripping everywhere. An arm shot out and hit Willem in the thigh, surprising him as he stepped back, and thankfully he didn't look up as Cec turned. Instead, Willem threw himself forward, toppling the man over so he fell sideways. Willem kept hitting the man's head with the candlestick, before moving forward and ramming the object into the hand that had dared to defile Cornelia. He heard distant shouts and feet running on the floor, and he saw moving shadows around himself until someone finally dragged him off the limp body of Cec. The feeling of having his arms held behind him made him cuss at the one doing it, twisting with desperation to get free — to reach the drowning Claes.

"Willem, stop," Cornelia told him.

Claes? Willem thought. He *had* reached Claes. Willem stopped resisting. Saw Cornelia in front of him, her face worried, not afraid. She should be afraid of the man on the floor, not worried for Willem.

As if the man had heard the thought, he groaned and began getting to his knees. Willem screamed at them to watch out as he saw it. Could Cec control them all at once?

He never found out. Cornelia turned around to see the man try to compose himself. She called forth her gift, the light only emanating from her right hand now. She clenched her fist and hit Cec in the back, sending him sprawling to the floor. Willem had never seen a woman do such a thing and he found himself smiling a vicious smile in surprise and relief at the same time. He barely registered Andries letting go of him, and his vision was pulled away from Cornelia as Alice grabbed hold of him, turning him towards her. He stared numbly into her face, his blood cooling now. Alice was still beautiful; fine lines like cobwebs, not the deep grooves he saw in so many elder ones. Alice took his face in both her hands, her smiling visage mixed with sadness.

"Thank you," she whispered, almost in tears, grateful she had not lost two grandchildren in as many days.

After only two nights in Alice's house, leaving it to finally conduct his father's business felt like stepping into another world, but there had been no way to avoid it. The Van Baas home had turned out to be a lovely little house outside the city. Upon his arrival, Willem was shown into a parlor that told him much about the tulip grower and his wife. Mrs. Van Baas took pride in her husband's reputation and growing fortune as his flowers gained a high reputation indeed with each season. Willem noted two paintings hanging on the wall signed by a young up-and-coming painter who would likely surpass Van Baas in fame in a few years no doubt. The parlor was furnished with luxurious furniture, the wood polished and waxed so it gleamed in the light that entered through a window. There was a pleasant warmth coming from the fireplace, tended to by a servant, Willem supposed, not Mrs. Van Baas herself. Not anymore. He could see shallow traces on the wooden floors and walls the previous furniture had left, forever marked by the sunlight. The tulip cultivation and trade had elevated their status. As if to inform every visitor of that fact, a neat bouquet of the famed flower stood in a vase on a table in the center of the room. It wasn't the most expensive kind; those were for trade, but it was a striking bouquet of red tulips that had begun spreading their petals.

"Are they not lovely?" Mrs. Van Baas asked as she walked towards the table and bent to peer at them as if she couldn't see them anytime she wished.

"They most certainly are a vision, Mrs. Van Baas," Willem said and walked over. The pain in his chest had eased much since the day before, leaving nothing more than a slight itch in his throat now. Alice had been right in asking him to stay another night so she could treat him with her horrible mixture of spices and medicines. It made it easier not to burst into a harrowing coughing-fit while a guest in someone's home.

"Evert grows them under glass," Mrs. Van Baas continued happily. "That's how we can enjoy them even at this time of year."

Willem nodded. As with a sinking city, one could circumspect Mother Nature herself by wrangling the magnificent science hidden within her, understand it and utilize it. That was how one ended up with canals cutting through a vibrant city, as well as tulips that would bloom even in January. No wonder the Van Baas home had seen financial changes in a short time! Willem noted the dark-blue silk dress on Mrs. Van Baas, the dark color of her bodice interspersed with black velvet. It would not have surprised him in the least if these textiles had passed through his father's warehouse before ending up out here where such dresses were not an everyday garment.

"Tell me, Mrs. Van Baas," he asked the older woman, "What occupation did your husband have before venturing into tulip cultivation?"

"Oh, my Evert was a clerk for Reinier Kuiper, you know, the famous lawyer," she said with conviction.

Willem nodded. He had never heard of the man and doubted he was, or ever had been, famous.

"But he did actually study botany in his youth. It has served him well now."

"Ah," Willem smiled at the flowers. The color was magnificent and flawless, and yet not as striking as the soft red glow that had emanated from Cornelia when she had used her gift to save him. Now that was beauty. "It certainly has served him well," he agreed with Mrs. Van Baas. "I hardly dare think of the beauty of the *Magna Avaritia* when it blooms."

"It's a masterpiece to behold, Mynheer De Meer. It truly is." Mrs. Van Baas shook her head almost in disbelief. She must, of course, have seen the flower up close. White as snow, his father had said, and with streaks of purple so dark it could be mistaken for black. Now such a thing would be a sight to behold. Even Willem had to admit to that, but he couldn't shake his father's teachings, and paying the last Florins he had for a mere flower? Well, that seemed like true folly.

"It's why my husband chose that name, you know. Everyone will want it, long to behold its beauty. So many already desire it. Wait until the flower grows in the spring," Mrs. Van Baas continued in her enthralled reverie of the flower. "Your house will be the place to be, your name the talk of the city."

Willem only smiled. The flower would never grow anywhere near his father's house. It would be sold for the largest sum of money they could obtain, and hopefully, save them from ruin. Enjoy its beauty? No, there would be none of that.

A dog's sharp bark somewhere in the house disturbed the calm and startled Mrs. Van Baas.

"Oh, I'm sorry. With Evert in the... I need to take care of that," she said and excused herself, leaving Willem to wait alone. He didn't mind. He had wondered if there were any dogs in Van Baas' household. He had not been able to see anything as he came to the house, but he had heard that the tulip growers had all kinds of traps and alarms in their gardens. That included large dogs that kept a vigil at night. That was necessary even in winter of course, when the bulbs lay under the frozen earth, like hidden treasures. The house of a tulip grower had to be a target for those not willing to buy the little gems as well. Thieves and burglars had no reservations in stealing flowers, when the flowers were worth more than jewels. The thought made him think of Cornelia, almost forced into thievery by Cec. He wondered how they could reason with such a man as that. The last he had seen of him was when Andries had dragged his lifeless body out of Cornelia's sewing room. She lived for that dream, didn't she? She had even managed to get her hands on good quality fabrics. Willem had noticed that in his befuddled state afterward. But she could not afford the true luxury textiles needed for a dressmaker of high class. If she wanted the richest ladies of Amsterdam as her customers, she needed the finest textiles. But she was working hard, he could see that with different orders that were almost finished in her little room. He had also noticed, upon leaving Alice's house late last night, the stone sign fastened on the façade of the building. It showed a pair of scissors, announcing the tailoring business within. Cornelia had a true driving force within her, and Willem found he admired that. It was something he missed in himself on those few occasions where he allowed himself to think about it.

The door behind him opened a little less quietly than when Mrs. Van Baas had gone through it. Willem turned to see Evert Van Baas himself, glad for the intrusion into his own troubled mind. Van Baas was a large man, broad-shouldered, yet slim around the waist. He had the physique of a man who worked in manual labor, but Willem suspected it was due to all the extra work he had to do to secure his merchandise. It was not lost on Willem that Mrs. Van Baas had stopped herself mid-sentence when almost stating where her husband had gone after Willem showed up. He likely had a hidden vault somewhere where he stored his precious tulips. Willem remembered a neighbor from his childhood in the city, a Mynheer Vinke. The man had hated anything on two legs, shouting at children for playing in the street, snarling at women and barking at men. He had cared for nothing but his dogs. Once, one late summer evening, Willem and Geert had once seen the foul old man crying as one of his dogs had been found dead on his front step. The mystery of who had hurt the animal had never been solved, but to Willem and Geert the angry man's crying had been a larger mystery indeed. Van Baas, in his brusque manner, struck Willem to be much like Mynheer Vinke, in his obvious fanaticism for the one thing he cared about. There was nothing more important than the tulips, his famed name more important than the riches they brought. Mrs. Van Baas likely bothered staying on account of their elevated status.

"Your father bid obsessively for this," Van Baas said as he showed Willem a small package. "He made a good deal. There is no more beautiful flower than this in the country." There was no modesty in his voice, only an obvious belief that he was right. Willem wasn't so certain though. There were many an *admirael* this or *generael* that out there, and a never-ending array of claims to their overpowering beauty. What mattered most to Willem now, was what others thought about the thing. It needed to fetch a good price.

"I'm sure my father knows exactly what he's doing."

"It's the same to me," Van Baas said. "I don't care if you sell it, but make sure it's done the right way," he said and sounded like his wife's complete opposite. "I'll not have any disgruntled buyers coming to my door because you made a bad deal. If you sell it on, make sure it's ironclad." He might love his flowers and fame, but he had no illusions when it came to the market he provided goods for.

"I assure you, Mynheer... the De Meer name has never been associated with shady deals." *Only unfortunate ones now*, Willem thought. "You will not hear of such a thing because of my father."

Willem arrived back in the city, early the next day. Having spent the night on his journey in a decent boarding house, he was still happy to come home despite the misfortune that was happening to his family there. Still, he had to admit to himself, that most of his happiness was due to his first stop in the city. Young Lieve had delivered Willem's message to Hendrika, and so he assumed he had not been expected back as soon as had first been the plan. So, when Alice had asked him to stop by her house upon his return, he had promised he would. He might have slept better in the feathered bed in the boarding house, but the thought of seeing Cornelia again spiraled that thought away, and he walked with an easy step. He didn't even let the small fortune currently resting in a pocket weigh him down as he navigated the streets. He crossed a few canals and generally enjoyed the cold day, with the sun peeking out now and then between tall and narrow houses to warm his face.

His good spirits were, however, forgotten as he walked along a canal not far from Alice's house. There was a commotion by the edge of the canal as a group of men worked hard to fish a dead body out of the water. A small crowd surrounded them, curious as to what kind of person had met his end in the cold embrace of the city's veins this night.

Willem froze as he realized what was happening. He had seen this many times before. Drunkards that fell in and couldn't get out, people who fell in by accident, or jumped in on purpose, those who were thrown in... Willem swallowed hard and tried walking on. This happened all the time. There was nothing unusual about it, was there? Willem had even jumped into one a few nights ago himself, but that had been under unusual circumstances.

His steps were slow, and he felt himself more drawn to the onlooking crowd than wanting to run away. A rush of water and then, "Yes, yes, we have him. All of you, pull," stopped him short. They were using a long pole with a hook on the end as well as a rope to get the poor floating bastard out of the water and up past the wall. The men heaved rhythmically at the rope. Soon a shade became visible for the onlookers between the men's legs as the deceased was pulled over the low wall on their end. He landed with a thump, and water poured everywhere around him. There was a lot of fabric, but that was due to his heavy cloak, not skirts. No, from what little Willem could see, it was definitely not a woman.

"Poor bastard. He froze to death down there, didn't he?" a man near Willem said as the surge of anticipation went through the small crowd. More and more seemed to join.

"Surely he drowned?" another said.

"Doesn't matter," a third joined in. "He's with the Lord now. The outcome is always the same."

Surprised shouting erupted around the body as they turned him over. Then a frenzied conversation began before several of them shrugged.

"All right," one of the officials shouted. "Anyone here know this man?"

The crowd sidled closer as if they were a joined entity. Everyone wanted to see, but no one wanted to be involved. Willem moved with them, less because he wanted to now, and more because he was trapped among them. Under his cloak, he moved his hand to rest around the packet containing the tulip bulb. The last thing he needed was for it to be stolen by a pickpocket.

The usual scent of urine and vomit was not particularly present as it had all frozen. Thus, the weak and uncomfortable smell of the dead body reached his nose as they stepped close enough to see. Willem stared in silence. He did know that man. Soaking wet, pale and limp. The chestnut hair plastered to his head, eyes open and staring ahead at something no one else could see. Cec's lips were parted, and there was a smile of sorts, but not on his mouth. The red gaping wound stretched from ear to ear, the color a stark contrast to the rest of him and everything else around him at the moment. Whatever blood there had been must have washed away in the ice-cold water.

Cec was dead. Willem was surprised at the initial relief he felt at that. No longer would Cornelia suffer from his threats. But dead? Who had done it? This was a murder. Cec had not done this to himself. He had been the type to hurt others, not himself. And the cut was deep, Willem had no trouble seeing that.

"Well?" the official shouted. "Anyone know him?"

No one answered. Even if there were anyone in the crowd who knew him besides Willem, they would surely know it was best to stay out of it.

"Then don't hang about here," the official shouted and began shooing them away.

The crowd slowly dispersed, and Willem continued on his route towards Alice's house. The last time he saw Cec alive, was when Andries had dragged him out of the room. The man had been busy with his heavy task, and no one had questioned what he was doing. Who was Andries really? Willem still hadn't found out what kind of familial connection he had to the rest of them, except for his brother Arend. Willem had asked Cornelia about it after dinner the second day of his stay in Alice's house, but the answer had left him none the wiser.

"Oh, Andries? He looks out for us. He... mends things." Cornelia had said, pausing her sewing of what Willem had thought to be a cap.

"Mends things?"

"Sometimes we get into trouble—"

"Or we create it," Marien had interrupted with a snort.

"Yes," Cornelia had agreed with a smile. "And so we have Andries to mend it for us."

Which had only confused Willem more. *Mend* things? How was killing a man mending something? Of course, the man in question had been dangerous, even with what Cornelia deemed a weak gift. Was this how they dealt with their problems? They were strong, he knew that. Their various talents were not something he had even thought possible on this earth. Considering what they could do, he wondered if they were invincible. Cec had clearly not been. Even Willem himself had managed to get the better of him, but that had been in an inattentive moment for the thief. Willem shook his head as he walked, hand still on the tulip parcel in his pocket. He could still hardly believe what had come over him. It was something he kept downtrodden and well hidden. Geert would never have approved. But there was nothing left for him to approve. Unless this flower saved them, there would be nothing for his father to be proud of. He would leave nothing behind when he died. Only a name that was worthless. No wonder the tulip growers named their damned flowers after themselves.

Admirael de Baas. Willem scoffed at the thought. The man was many things, but not that.

He walked on until a simple sign brought forth a smile on his lips again; a pair of scissors carved in stone. As he knocked, he thought it strange that his father's house never brought such a feeling anymore.

The door opened to reveal Cornelia, a half sewn dark green bodice in her hand that she had forgotten to leave in her sewing room. At the sight of him, her whole face broke into a smile, so warm and welcoming. Was this what it was like, Willem wondered, to be truly welcomed and wanted somewhere? He couldn't help but reciprocate.

"Enough with the doe eyes, you two," Alice's voice broke in before either of them could say anything. Willem had lost his voice anyway, as the old woman stepped forward to pull him into the house.

"I couldn't have planned your visit better if I tried," she said.

"Oh?" he managed.

"I have a surprise for you, young man. A gift, for all you have done for us." She stopped a moment as she frowned. "Is something wrong?"

Willem remembered Cornelia's comment about wishing to have inherited her Grandmother's gift; how she could sense what others felt.

He shook his head. "Everything's fine, Mrs. Aarden. I

was just thinking of an old memory. Not a good one, but it cannot be changed."

Alice nodded and her smile returned, though a little less joyful.

"I understand. The past can be painful. I have lost children myself. I recognize the pain of loss."

Willem simply nodded. He didn't want to talk about his brother now. Not when Cornelia had met him with such a smile.

"So," Alice continued. "I have a gift for you."

"That's not nes—"

"Nonsense," she waved him off. "It is my pleasure."

"But you saved my life, that's enough for—"

"And you saved both my grandchildren. Both without knowing, and while knowing about us." She patted him on the cheek like only older women can do. "That is a rare thing. Not everyone takes kindly to us when exposed to us."

"I..."

"Never mind. Such dark truths. Please indulge an old grandmother. I will fetch the gift," she added before he could answer and then turned on her heel before she disappeared into the house.

"Most people find it best to go with what Oma says," Cornelia said behind him. He turned to find her standing by the door, still with the half-finished bodice in her hands.

"I disturbed you," he said, nodding to the green garment.

She smiled.

"Never." Her long hair was pulled back into a loose braid. He wondered why she preferred it hanging freely instead of tucked under a cap. He longed to be allowed to ask such personal things. He should have done so during the night they had spent in the alcove. It seemed such rules had been suspended then.

"I'll just put this back," Cornelia said, indicating the bodice. "Then I'll take you through. Oma's gift is special. It can be difficult as well, but that depends on what one does with it."

As he waited, the smell of tobacco, earthy and dry, reached Willem before Yorov himself did.

"Heard you'd come back, boy," he said and chuckled before putting the clay pipe back in his mouth. The pipe was whiter than the smoke that rose from it in gray tendrils. He must have found it wherever he had mislaid it. "One night with Lia not enough, eh? Didn't think she'd be that interesting to tell the truth." He guffawed at that.

"I'll mind you not to talk that way about—"

"Don't bother with him, Wim," Cornelia said as she exited her sewing room. "He's only a miserable old man."

Yorov showed his yellowed teeth. It reminded Willem of one of Mynheer Vinke's dogs. "You should watch your mouth, Lia."

"Or what?" she said, as a flicker of the red-golden light crossed her face. "You'll treat me like one of the daughters that provide for you?"

Yorov pressed his lips together a moment, before taking a drag of his pipe again.

"Good luck with that one," he said and headed for the door. Cornelia huffed as it closed behind him.

"Probably going to a tavern for the night."

"It's midday."

"Exactly," she said, an annoyed frown on her face.

"What's with his daughters?"

"He's disappointed in their lack of... his ability. They have weaker gifts, inherited from their mother, the poor woman," she added and visibly shuddered at the thought of being married to the man. She took Willem's hand in hers and led him through the house, towards the backroom that housed the large kitchen and eating table. It was clearly the heart of the home.

"Why do you let him stay here?" Willem asked, enjoying the gentle squeeze of her hand.

Cornelia shrugged.

"He's part of our community."

"Was Cec?"

Cornelia stopped and looked at him. They were standing close together in a narrow hallway that opened up by his alcove and led into the kitchen. There was a pleasant smell of food. Meat and vegetables? Something was cooking in there at least.

"What do you mean *was*?" Cornelia asked him.

"He's dead."

Cornelia nodded. There was a faint hint of surprise on her face, but also a look that said she had expected it.

"He was an affiliate... " she began. "But not all can claim that safety. Not when they repeatedly threaten it."

Willem nodded, was about to say something, and then promptly forgot. He looked at her where she stood so close, their fingers still entwined. She was looking at him in a most curious way, eyes open and honest, full lips barely parted. He wanted nothing more than to kiss her. Did she want the same? She was not stepping away. Instead, she took a step closer, and—

"Lia, don't be so slow!" a voice shouted so they could hear it in the other end of the house. It startled them both, and Cornelia rolled her eyes before she smiled; the infectious beautiful smile.

"All right, Marien. No need to shout." Cornelia tugged at Willem's hand and he followed her into the kitchen.

"What's going on?" he asked as he was guided to a chair by the table. He sat down and was pleased that Cornelia sat down next to him. It was a large square table which seated ten people on a regular basis with the two households.

Every time Willem had been there though, there had always been four extra chairs, which indicated a regular stream of guests at their meals. Had he not been one himself?

"Sometimes we give back to those who help us," Cornelia explained. "That includes our own leaders and menders, but they have to prove themselves first. Oma is satisfied you have done that."

Willem had no idea what that meant and settled for waiting to see. There were so many new things with these people, things that were not supposed to be possible. It was best to simply go with it.

So he sat at the table and talked to Cornelia and Marien who walked about the kitchen, tending to a stew that simmered over the fire. When the figure of Alice finally appeared, Willem glanced at the door with a smile.

"This is how you support your community, my dear. We all protect and help each other," she was saying to someone behind her. As she entered the kitchen, Willem saw Andries following her, and his smile faltered. He remembered the dead body on his way there, and despite not liking the thief, hating him actually, he realized he had become weary of Andries. He didn't even know what ability the man had besides cutting a man's throat.

Which was why he didn't notice the third person walking in the door at first. She wore a lovely dark-green dress. It had white and silver threads sewn into the bodice, and the intricate lace collar and cap. It was not something one expected to see in Alice's house. Willem looked up to meet his fiancée Catharijn's startled face.

All in all, it took Willem a few minutes to grasp the situation. That did however not make it any less confusing for him.

"What on earth's the matter with you?" Alice asked Catharijn as she'd stopped dead in the doorway. Willem noticed her hand slide out of Andries' grasp, and her eyes moving away from him. Whatever she had expected, it had not been Willem. Nor had he expected her. She was a merchant's daughter. What was she doing running around the streets of Jordaan? It was no place for her. And why was she in this particular house?

"Are you all right, dear?" Alice asked as she stepped closer. Catharijn managed to pull herself together as a blank mask fell over her face.

"I'm fine. I am simply not comfortable with an outsider here."

"Oh," Alice said. She seemed to have been confused by the array of emotions that had filled the room a moment ago. Willem tried to collect himself as best he could as well. It was clear that there was something going on between his fiancée and Andries. Stolen glances and the now separated hands spoke volumes. But Willem had known that, hadn't he? She had asked him to have his father break off their engagement because she wanted to get married to someone else. Willem had assumed she meant to marry someone of her own station. If he read her correctly now, she planned on marrying down. Why though? Wait. Outsider? Willem was one, and she was not?

That could only mean one thing — she was one of them. She had an ability as well. Willem was about to ask her when he remembered himself. Catharijn had deflected Alice's question. She didn't want them to know. Whether she didn't want to reveal she was already engaged, or if it were only whom she was engaged to... well, either way, she wanted Willem to keep quiet. He glanced at Cornelia who watched this little entrance with confusion as well. He didn't mind keeping quiet he realized. That was better than any misunderstanding. Such things could be handled later.

He hoped there would be a later.

"Willem," Alice said, drawing him back to the situation at hand. "This is Catharijn van Heuvel. She is part of our community, and she will provide you with your reward."

Willem managed a neutral greeting as Catharijn came further into the room. Andries remained by the door.

"I really don't need a reward," Willem tried again.

"Nonsense. We must pay our debts when they accumulate. And I can never truly do that seeing as what you gave me was life itself in my two grandchildren." Willem noticed young Claes was still bedridden in a narrow and movable bed not far from the oven. But he seemed alert enough as he leaned halfway over the edge to get a peek at what was going on.

Catharijn, reluctantly, sat down at the table, gathering her expensive skirts around her as she moved the chair closer to the table. A few blond curls framed her face and didn't quite hide the blood that went to her cheeks.

"Don't worry," Willem found himself saying without thinking. "Your secret is safe with me."

She looked up then and smiled a weak smile. It was a smile nonetheless, and it seemed to ease her tension somewhat.

Alice mouthed a silent "thank you" behind Catharijn as she grabbed a chair and sat down as well. "Catharijn here has been blessed with the sight."

"The what?" Willem asked, and immediately felt like an idiot as everyone else nodded along with Alice as if this were common knowledge.

"The sight. She has the gift of seeing what may be."

"Not *may* be. All of it comes to fruition," Catharijn herself chimed in.

Alice nodded and smiled at her.

"What will be," she amended. "If there is anything you want to know, she will see how it unfolds for you."

"But that's not possible," Willem blurted. He was still in shock from even seeing this woman here, and the feeling was mutual. "See the future?"

"Only certain and specific glimpses of it," Catharijn said. She didn't want him to know about it, but since he now did, it had to be the truth.

"Don't be so quick to claim what's possible," Alice said. "What have you seen these past few days?"

Willem looked at Cornelia again. Reddish-golden light of pure strength. As he turned back, he saw a distinct, small and knowing smile on Catharijn's lips. She had seen in Willem what he saw in her when looking at Andries. That seemed to settle it, for her reluctance vanished. She now wanted to be done with it.

"But there is no need... " he tried one last time.

"You may not have our talents," Alice said, "but you have earned our gratitude."

"Now... is there anything in your life you want to know about?"

Images flashed through Willem's mind. Cornelia's beautiful smile, the near kiss they'd shared. Cornelia pulling Willem and Claes out of the canal, that warm and glowing light. The canal brought back images of his dying brother. The crowd looking down and yelling, cheering. There was nothing more to see from that. No more future. His father's illness. Their misfortune.

"An object will help me focus," Catharijn said as an afterthought. They all waited for him to make a decision. Slowly, and without thinking too much about it, Willem pulled the small packet from his pocket and put it on the table.

"Can you read something off of this?" he asked and pushed the thing towards Catharijn with his index finger. Maybe, if what she claimed were true, she could find out if it would save them. If it could save his father before it was too late. Before his reputation was ruined.

Catharijn pulled the packet towards herself and, with a questioning look towards Willem who nodded his consent, she opened it. She searched through bits of straw used for padding before she withdrew a tulip bulb. It was no beauty now, merely a brown round thing, pointy in one end and resembling an onion more than anything. But they all knew what it was. A gasp went around the table. It had to be one of the expensive ones since Willem had traveled personally outside the city to get it. That much was obvious to them. But he didn't fear they would try and steal it. He had learned they were honest folk. Otherwise, he would likely have been found in a canal with a slit throat by now as well.

Catharijn took the bulb in her hand and closed her eyes a moment. She didn't say or do anything else for a long time and they all sat there in silence. Then her eyes began fluttering under her eyelids. Willem wondered if she were dreaming or simply seeing something disturbing.

When she opened her eyes again, Willem noticed Marien stepping back. She had great respect for this gift, and it didn't matter that it was intangible.

"I have grave news for you," Catharijn said as she put the bulb back into the straw. "I see a great beauty, with striking colors, flawless, the envy of growers, especially because of one of the colors."

"But?" Willem said, entranced despite his initial doubts.

"I also see them falling. All of them. In a matter of days, you might as well eat it."

"What?"

"The new month will barely have begun, and then it will be too late."

The new month? Willem looked at her with disbelief. Not in her sight. No, he believed that. How could he not when he had seen so many impossible things in this house?

"You mean to say the tulips will be worthless?" Andries asked her.

Catharijn nodded without looking back.

"The craze will cool, and the fame of the beauties will be forgotten."

Willem suddenly felt his pulse in his ears. January was at its end. How could this be? He had gotten the tulip. Fetched it for his father. Their last hope. Now there would only be destitution waiting. Nothing to take pride in. No name to show worth. Nothing.

※ 14 ※

The tavern was lively with talk and song. A few patrons had even begun dancing as a small crowd cheered them on. They clapped the rhythm for the couples moving about, swinging their bodies on the floor. The drink was plentiful, and the tobacco smoke hung low in the tap room. In one corner a man puked up the drink he could no longer hold down. One of the serving maids let him have it, as she was the one who had to clean it up. Willem barely noticed as he had retreated to a corner, a jug of beer on the table by him: untouched and forgotten. He had left Alice's house shortly after Catharijn's prediction. He needed to think. How could he bring the bulb to his father now? The deal was dead. They needed to bide their time to fetch the best price possible. He glanced up as a man whispered something to a man by a door that led into one of the back-rooms. A password most likely. The tulip market could be found in many a tavern, but to sell this particular bulb one could not go anywhere. And not at any time either. The prices fluctuated greatly and the difference between two nights could be several Florins indeed. What were they to do? They would have to take what they could get, and that might not be enough to start up the business from scratch again.

"Why, young cousin Wim," a familiar voice boomed as Willem looked up to see Little Pieter coming out of one of the back rooms. Little Pieter maneuvered his large frame between the tables that separated them and sat down at Willem's table without an invitation. Willem bit his teeth together while keeping his face neutral. Why now? Did the man always have to show up when Willem was the recipient of bad news? Could he sense it? Was Little Pieter drawn to his kin's misfortune like a mosquito to blood?

"I just made quite the profitable deal from my *Admirael de Baas*," he said and indicated the door to the backroom with his large head. He then scratched his beard while looking closer at Willem. "You seem out of spirits tonight. Something amiss?"

"No. Congratulations on your deal." Willem was surprised at how civil he managed to sound. Little Pieter could make a deal like that. Even if his tulip fetched a higher price the next night, he would not be in ruin because of it.

"So, how did your father's business go?"

Willem suddenly wanted to throw his beer in the man's face. Little Pieter could taunt and tease, but he seldom asked about such matters directly. Then it dawned on Willem that he was, in fact, inquiring about the *Magna Avaritia*, not the *Filomena*. They were in a tavern at the moment, but despite the singing, laughter and loud voices vying for attention, there could still be ears in such a place. Willem didn't wish for a second trip into a canal because someone got whiff of the potential fortune in his pocket.

"It went well," he told Little Pieter. "We have it and are now considering our options. It is, after all, a most prestigious thing." Willem felt the lies spill out of him, as they had from his father regarding his business. The least

Willem could do was maintain their pride until it truly was no more. Besides, the look of want and greed on Little Pieter's face gave him some satisfaction. At least for a little while, Willem's father had bested his cousin in procuring the most beautiful tulip.

A shout from the door drew Little Pieter's attention, a man Willem didn't recognize. Little Pieter gave a wave and stood.

"Well, give my best to your father. I saw him this morning, and he didn't look well."

As it turned out, Little Pieter was right. Willem returned home to the Keizersgracht late that night, smelling of tobacco and alcohol without having consumed much of anything himself. He had been met by De Vries who'd told him he was expected in his father's bedchamber. He had never been allowed in there as a child either. There were parts of the house that were Pieter de Meer's undisputed domain.

"Have you been spending all this time drinking?" His father's voice came with reproach, the sting hard as always despite his wheezing breath. Consumption, De Vries had said. *More than that*, Willem thought, as he gave in to the itch in his own throat and coughed instead of answering. Pieter de Meer looked a broken man where he lay in bed, covered by thick blankets. He was dressed in an intricately embroidered and expensive nightshirt. His pallid skin matched the white linen of his shirt. He was sweating and in need of the covers all the same. The room was sweltering with the heat from the lit fireplace.

"What does the doctor say?" Willem asked as he removed his jerkin and hung it on the back of the chair. That made it easier to bear the temperature. He was seated next to the bed and remained focused on his father's heavy and strained breathing. Out of the two of them, his father might as well have been the one who fell in the canal. No, it was not only consumption that rode his father's body; it was the collapse of their world. Their way of life.

"I cannot afford a doctor," Pieter said. "Nor can I afford rumors spreading about that."

Willem nodded. So to avoid debt and rumor, he had sacrificed his health.

"That's foolish." He heard the words leave his own mouth as in a dream. Saw his father's widened eyes at the impudence, and sat up in the chair.

"Maybe it is," Pieter said after a while. "But that is my choice."

"Yes, Father."

"I think it's time we face the truth of it all, Son."

No, Willem wanted to say. He didn't want that.

"These may be my last days," Pieter went on. "Things have gone downhill lately. It all fell apart when Geert was taken from me."

Willem stiffened in the chair. Geert should never have died. That had been Willem's responsibility. The likable, clever and hard-working Geert. Loved and admired by all. Always with an easy smile.

"You were supposed to aid your brother in what is to come, to look out for him," Pieter said. It sounded factual, but Willem could not help but hear the slight touch of reproach in his voice. He inhaled deeply, the smell of the fire, his father's sour sweat, the tobacco smoke from the tavern infused in his own clothes — it was all nauseating. It had always been his charge to look out for Geert. Willem might have been the youngest, but because of that, they had different responsibilities when it came to the family and the business.

"I know that," Willem said, his voice so contrite it almost hurt to get the words out.

"Geert was a good boy," Pieter said. "To kill him for

trying to right a wrong... a father should not live to see such a thing."

Willem had seen it. He had been there. He would never forget how his good-spirited brother had stepped in to stop a fight between two men outside a tavern. How they had turned on him with all their friends. Willem had tried to help him, but they had held him back. They had twisted his arms behind his back until they almost broke. And then they had lifted Geert up and thrown him in the canal, cheering in their drunken stupor as he drowned. Geert had been too drunk himself to manage to stay afloat. It hadn't mattered that the water hadn't been freezing; it had been deep enough to swallow Geert.

"I miss him so much," Pieter said.

So do I, Willem wanted to say. But he remained quiet. He had never seen his father like this. He had always been unyielding, decisive and quick to act. Set in his ways perhaps, but a ruthless survivor. Geert's death seemed to have finally killed most of his spirit.

"Do you have the tulip? The *Magna Avaritia?*"

"I have it right here."

"Then you must sell it."

"I?"

"I wish I could leave this to Geert, I do, but you must take his place now, Wim. You must save the company and run it. At least until I am well again."

If that even happens, Willem thought, as his father tried to inhale deeply. It was like he was trying to suck clay through a straw.

"The tulip market will crash."

"What?"

"You heard me."

"That's nonsense. People are mad for the flowers. There are those who earn enough to buy large houses. Even in our neighborhood. They earn several years' wages in one single deal."

"And yet it will end."

"When?"

"All too soon."

"Then you must hurry. But be sure you make a profit."

"But—"

"I don't care how" Pieter raised his voice to a near shout. "Don't make a mess of this as you did with your brother," he snapped. The exertion of his outburst caused a nasty cough that lasted long enough for Willem to calm down from the angered guilt that flared up in him. Pieter turned over on his side, breathing hard until his lungs would let him speak again.

"Where have you been these past few days?" he asked, not finished with the admonishments.

Somewhere without these obligations, Willem thought. Somewhere where he was met with the loveliest smile when he knocked on the door. Somewhere where he could be needed for who he was, not who he was needed to be. Somewhere where someone had his back. If he dared take the chance. He didn't want this, he realized, as he looked at his father's ailing frame. Thin and weak. Yet still strong in there. Fighting until the end. Willem respected that. And Pieter was right as well. Willem should have protected Geert better. Should have fought harder, despite the odds. Despite the fact that there had been twelve men against the two of them. If he'd had a gift like Cornelia and her kin... think of what he could have done then. Geert would have been alive, and his father would have been well and happy, even with Willem. It was such gifts that they passed on to their children. They might be hiding, keeping to themselves, but they had ways of protecting themselves. How he wished for that as he received his father's admonishments! But it had never been given to either him or

Geert. It was not in their parents' blood. They had Pieter's textile business, once grand and now rotting on the bottom of the ocean.

"Sell it as quick as you can," Pieter repeated. "It's our only hope."

Willem heard footsteps behind him. It could only be his father's servant, De Vries. He often showed up unannounced like that, as if he could sense his master's need for him.

"De Vries will help you. You can trust him."

Willem didn't turn. Didn't wish to see the bony face of the man, the little knowing smile that seemed to question everything Willem did. Or wasn't capable of, in the servant's opinion. It was never expressed out loud of course. That was not a servant's place. One thing was for certain: De Vries would be the first to go if Pieter died. Willem would rather have no servant than that servant.

"I can't simply begin to make deals in your name."

"I have signed the necessary papers, boy. Use the tulip while you still can. And change your clothes. That infernal smell of tobacco bothers me."

15

Willem fumed in silence as he walked blindly through the streets, tall narrow houses in neat rows, passed him by as mere shadows around him. He had not slept that night; his father's scorn repeating itself in his head. All the things he had wanted to say. All the things he could not defend himself against. All the things that made him question his father's words. How could that even be? Was it because he had experienced a different way of seeing family in Alice's house?

De Vries walked beside him in silence. Willem was glad of that at least. He didn't want to talk to him. Had nothing to talk about with him. The man's so-called loyalty didn't extend beyond Willem's father, did it? He could not be trusted. Still, that didn't stop the man from finally saying something as they approached the harbor and neared the warehouse.

"Who's that?" De Vries asked and nodded towards a figure walking outside the warehouse. A man looked up at the sign on the front, which stated the name of the company that owned it.

With all the worries in his head, it took Willem a

moment to recognize the unkempt and lanky frame of Yorov as he took in the multi-storied building. What was he doing there? Checking up on Willem?

"No one," he said to De Vries and told him to stay back as Willem walked up to Yorov.

"What are you doing here?" he demanded of him.

Yorov turned and feigned surprise, an exaggerated grimace so bad it was hard to believe he even bothered with it. "Why, what a surprise to see you here, boy! Thought I recognized the name." He indicated the De Meer name in its large letters above the doors.

"Are you following me?"

Yorov smiled at that, and Yorov's smile was not a nice one, more like a sneer; like an animal baring its teeth when threatened.

"Why would I do that?"

"Oh, I'm sure you know about the tulip by now." The man lived in the same household that had seen the bulb, and though Willem didn't suspect any of them to try something, he had no such illusions about this man.

Yorov simply shrugged.

"I also heard it won't be worth much for much longer."

Willem forced a smile on his lips. He was sure it was as fake as Yorov's.

"Well, don't you worry about that. It's been sold. So there is no need for you to snoop around my warehouse."

"Oh, so it's *your* warehouse? I thought your father was the rich one."

"What do you want, Yorov?" Willem pressed, clenching his fists and struggling to keep calm. There were people milling about everywhere. Losing his composure now would not help to keep a low profile until salvation or bankruptcy. Seagulls cried out above them, drawn to the busy area, searching for discarded scraps of food. The noise grated on Willem.

"Nothing from you, Mynheer de Meer," Yorov snarled, his usual assumed friendliness gone now. He didn't like being caught, especially when doing something shady. "You miserable fool," he added for good measure.

"Then I'd appreciate you moving away from my property," Willem said and made a quick shooing motion with a hand.

"You think you're so much better than me, don't you?" Yorov snarled and stepped closer instead of doing as told. "You come into our house, eat our food, and lay your eyes on our women like you can have what you want."

"Our?" Willem managed as he struggled not to gag from the man's sour breath. Despite the foul odor of stale food, sour tobacco and alcohol, he stood his ground.

Yorov scoffed at his comment, which only made the smell worse.

"I don't see you rushing down here to do business. We're in the forenoon now, but everyone else is here early each morning, and look," he added, theatrically indicating the area around them. "Business is flourishing everywhere but in this building."

There was no denying that. People came and went from every warehouse around them. There was a stream of vendors as well, selling or being chased away from the same houses. Nothing took place in front of the De Meer building.

"And you have your sights on Lia, huh? What do you even have to offer? Accusing me... *me* of snooping around your property; well what about you?"

"She's not your property, you fool."

"She is one of us. And you are nothing." Yorov spit the words out. Indignation apparent in his reddened face, he had little but pride. "You may think your name provides for you, but we both know what I can do to you if I so choose." He raised a hand but didn't let his ability show. Not outside in a public place. But Willem had seen enough in Alice's courtyard.

"Get out of here, Yorov. You're not welcome."

"You do not come in and take one of our own. Your blood is worthless, and seemingly your name as well."

"And still I have what you don't," Willem said, a small smile on his lips, despite his lies. "A name of worth. Respect. Everything you want."

"And how long will that last?" Yorov asked as he finally stepped back a little. Angry, and with his damned smile, he found his bottle in his pocket again and took a deep swig of the liquid. "I wish you a splendid day, Mynheer," he said as he made a mock bow and withdrew from the warehouse. He sauntered away, and made unwanted comments to any passersby who in turn shied away from him.

"You should be wary of that one," De Vries' voice came so unexpectedly that it made Willem jump. He turned to see the man had come closer, though he didn't know how much he'd heard.

"He's no one."

"That's a mistaken assumption to make of anyone."

Willem eyed the servant, whose face was partly shaded under a hat brim.

"Never mind him. Let's just get through this day."

16

Yorov's harsh words did nothing to ease Willem's mind, nor
were they meant to. He rummaged around the warehouse
to take stock of what little was left and found nothing of
worth. A few Florins altogether: nothing that would pay for
more than a little food. Soon they would need that. He
would take De Vries with him to the taverns tonight to sell
the damned bulb. The thing still rested in his pocket, and it
felt heavier and heavier as the hours wore on. No matter
the price, he would be glad to be rid of the thing.

"Why did my father spend his last money on such a
venture?" he asked De Vries after a long time of silent
work. Yorov's words bothered him, more than he wanted to
admit, and he didn't want to think on them. With no good
name, no fortune, no respect and certainly no ability...
maybe he was no good for Cornelia. She was special, even
in terms of her own kind. He stood with an old roll of soft
blue silk. How he wished to drape Cornelia in silks of red
and gold, just like she could do herself! She was so beautiful, so fiery and driven in her dreams. How striking she
would look in the fabrics the De Meers had dealt in!

"It was a gamble," De Vries answered as he stopped

looking into chests that turned out to be empty. "The way he saw it, he had nothing to lose."

"He had the last of the money to lose."

"And everything to win. Tulipomania has enabled many people when it comes to favorable deals."

Willem stared at the silk and dropped it on the floor.

"It was foolish," he said, voice low, again not believing he had said that.

"What now?" De Vries said.

"Foolish," Willem repeated. "The prudent thing to do would be to start anew with what little he had, make use of his contacts and get on with it." Willem drew breath, glanced at De Vries, and then exhaled slowly. The smile on the servant's face did not seem mocking. Why not?

"Your father has lived a long life, set in his ways perhaps. This was a last attempt to think in a new way."

"Long life? Him? And you're a young foal, are you?"

That actually did make De Vries smile properly. He closed the lid of the chest he'd been looking into, before sitting on it.

"My bones creak, certainly, but Leendert de Vries died decades ago. De Vries is but a mere ghost who has a debt to repay."

Willem blinked. It had never occurred to him, after his childhood at least, to think the man had a first name.

"Did my father save your life or the like?" he asked. He had no idea why the man was offering him information, but he was too curious to care.

"No. No lives were saved."

"So one was taken?"

De Vries shrugged, his dark eyes giving away nothing.

"Maybe I will tell you one day. But not today."

"Yes. We have business to take care of."

"Your brother's business?"

"Geert was a fool," Willem said and walked into his

father's upstairs office. Words of judgment had again fallen out of him. He felt like water boiling in a pot, unable to contain it all anymore. There were spills beyond his year-long control.

"Was he now?" De Vries said as he sauntered in behind him, uninvited.

"He was a fool. I loved him, but he was a damned fool," Willem said and sank into his father's chair. He didn't care that he was saying this to his father's loyal man. Let De Vries tell on him. Yorov was right. Willem was worth nothing in either world. He searched his father's desk.

"The right bottom drawer," De Vries said.

Sure enough, there Willem found the brandy bottle. He didn't care for a glass, simply drank straight from the bottle. The burning liquid spread a warmth through him that was calming and welcome.

"Geert was everything most people want to be," he said as De Vries leaned against the windowsill. "He made friends easily, had a kind and loving disposition, so smart it was frustrating. No wonder his studies were completed with ease. How I looked up to him!"

De Vries nodded. He knew this, having seen them grow up together.

"But he was a fool. Thinking he could settle a score between furious and drunk men. And all because he thought the world is better when people are peaceful. It wasn't the first time either, mind you." Willem pointed at the silent De Vries with the bottle and took another swig. It made him wince as it went down, but he liked it. "No. He did stupid things like that, and it got him killed. He had all of Father's talents, but not his cynicism and ruthlessness. Which have faded by the way. By God, the man's lack of imagination is what caused this, not Geert's pointless death."

Geert's idealism had been killed as assuredly as the men

had thrown him into the canal. Not that Willem disagreed with him, but people were people. Messy, cruel and vicious. *Not all, of course*, he thought bleakly as the image of Cornelia flashed before his mind. But you needed to see the real world for what it was and deal with it, not treat it as your own personal fantasy.

"Why do you say that?" De Vries asked, arms folded across his chest.

"Because his narrow focus is what caused this. What if he'd had stakes in other companies, bothered to invest in other goods? We may not have been filthy rich, but at least not on the brink of destitution." Willem drank again, and then realized he should stop. This was not the day to get drunk. He could drink himself into a stupor when it was all done. "Go find something useful to do, De Vries." He dismissed the man with a nod to the door and put the bottle back in the drawer. "You can wait," he mumbled and sat up, and then realized there was little for him to do. It would be the banks tomorrow. A task he did not relish. He had looked over his father's papers, and he knew the house would have to go. Like the one in Haarlem. His mother had loved that house. The thought made him cringe. Geert had taken after their mother. He'd had her kind and infectious disposition.

A knock on the door startled him.

"Damn it, De Vries. Can't you try and make a sound when you walk?"

"A visitor, Mynheer."

"What? *Here?*" Willem heard someone else's footsteps ascend the stairs. A visitor inside the warehouse meant a witness to their misfortune.

"A potential customer, I should say," De Vries said, his voice low so whoever it was couldn't hear. "At least for someone with an eye for reality."

Willem stared at him in surprise as the large frame of

Little Pieter became visible behind De Vries. "I'll leave you to it," he said as he stepped away. Willem glared after him a moment. Little Pieter was worse than a stranger bearing witness to the barren warehouse.

"Oh, Wim" he began as he walked into the office. It was not meant as a place to greet customers, and so there were no chairs for a guest to sit in. Willem didn't feel inclined to offer him one anyway. The game was up now. Truly. No more dancing around Little Pieter's suspicions.

"What misfortune has befallen you?" Little Pieter asked. "Where is Pieter?"

"He's very ill, Cousin."

"I feared as much. Are you in charge then?"

"I am."

"Can I do something to help? I can lend you some money. Or offer you a job."

And I will forever be indebted to you and you can hold it over my father's head, Willem thought darkly. He looked closer at Little Pieter. No, that was somewhat harsh. They were kin. But the little hint of a triumphant mask was there. It was what had made Willem's father lie to him about the situation the entire time. They had always been in competition, each Pieter trying to best the other for decades. It had driven them, and they had each lost and won throughout the years. *Foolish men*, Willem thought. Life was not a friendly game. You lived, you fought your way up, and you died. Suddenly he saw Yorov's haggard face spitting the words at him. *You are nothing.*

"I have no need of help, Cousin," Willem told Little Pieter. "As you know, my father made a wise decision on his last investment. It will fetch a few Florins, don't you think?"

"Ah... yes." Little Pieter licked his lips like a man longing for the finest wine. "The *Magna Avaritia*. The two-colored beauty."

"Yes. It will be the envy of the city for the lucky man who can buy it," Willem agreed and pulled the packet from his pocket. "You are family, so I trust I can show this to you," he said without looking up at Little Pieter.

"Of course," the man said and Willem noted his shadow falling on the desk as he couldn't help but step closer. Willem unpacked the bulb and put it on the desk.

"Imagine how something so simple can become so beautiful and be the envy of the whole city. To have its eyes on you the week it blooms."

"Quite the masterpiece" Little Pieter agreed as Willem looked up. It was clear to him that Little Pieter didn't share Mrs. Van Baas' devotion to the flower's beauty. No, Little Pieter was already thinking of the immense profit that could be made.

"Anyway," Willem said, raising his voice a little to shake his father's cousin out of his reverie. "De Vries and I will sell it tonight."

"Ah, but... "

"What?" Willem looked at the large man with the patient smile of a man who says he has business to tend to, and time is running short, you understand.

"Dealing with the bidding and selling of these flowers is strenuous, young Wim. One should not only stick to one of the taverns that deal in this market. You are inexperienced in this regard."

"I think I know how to conduct my business, Cousin."

"Oh, no doubt, no doubt. But I was thinking... "

"Yes?"

"I do have some experience in this... mayhap I can help you out?"

Willem sat back in his chair, as he feigned consideration.

"How so?"

"Let me buy it from you, and then it will be out of your hands. I can sell it on easily enough."

Willem thought for a moment, startled by a creak of a loose floorboard outside the office. De Vries was paying attention. Willem looked back at Little Pieter's face, seeing the greed so apparent there. This man could not mask anything well enough.

"February has begun," Willem whispered.

"What?"

Willem shook his head and smiled wider.

"Nothing, my dear cousin. Your offer is most kind. But mind you, I cannot skimp on the price. The value of this flowery jewel is too high."

"Oh, no. I understand," said Little Pieter already counting out in his head what profit he could stand to gain.

"Shall I send De Vries to fetch the lawyer then? To have proper papers drawn?"

Little Pieter grinned, not believing his luck. And it had all come from his cousin's misfortune.

Willem smiled back, as he called for De Vries.

An eye for reality indeed.

17

"You did what?" Pieter de Meer managed between his aching coughing-fits.

"You heard me," Willem said as he stood at the foot of his father's bed. The springs under the mattress creaked with the older man's involuntary movements.

"But Little Pieter?"

"He wanted it. He bought it. It's out of my hands."

"But you said the market will crash."

"Yes."

"How can you even know such a thing?"

"I just do." Willem couldn't tell the truth. His father would not believe him. No one would, and Willem couldn't fault anyone for that. Had he not seen what he'd seen himself, he would have thought everyone in Alice's house was mad.

Pieter began coughing again, drawing desperate breaths between the fits.

"Where is Hendrika with the damn tincture?"

"Asleep, Father."

"Asleep?

"It's the middle of the night. The night watchman

announced the hour not long ago. It's three o'clock, and besides, Hendrika is seventy-four."

Pieter growled and sank back in his bed.

"Have her make the swill first thing in the morning then. I can't sleep for this damn coughing."

"Of course." Willem waited patiently for the next bout to wear off.

"And the money?" Pieter asked, apparently there was little more concern for the buyer.

"All paid. Little Pieter is nothing if not efficient."

"Good. Now here's what I want you to do. There is a textile merchant in Haarlem that I have done business with before, and—"

"No," Willem broke in. It surprised him how calm he was. He wasn't even pretending anymore.

"Don't interrupt me, boy, I—"

"You named me Willem, Father. Use it. I said no. We are not going to keep falling into the same trap. Your tactics and plans may have worked for you in the past, but you've proved the fallibility of it yourself.

"Now listen here," Pieter began as he tried sitting up, which he did not manage.

"I will invest in sound merchandise. Trusted goods that people need and want, the risk spread out, so as not to lose it all in a few shipwrecks. Are we not part of the greatest trading nation?" Willem tilted his head a bit to the side as he considered his father's shocked stare. "I will attend the stock market as soon as possible and the money will be spent on gold and wine. Did you know the Baltic is pregnant with grain in the season, and the spices from the East are of the highest quality? Of course, we will deal in textiles, the finest silks and everything else. But I tell you one thing. There will be no more narrow-minded mistakes. I will use our name and our wealth and eventually our power as well.

When I need something, I will do as I did today and take it." He stopped again and smiled at his father, but there was no feigned kindness now, only the truth. "And you can lie here with your memory of foolish Geert who would likely have made the same mistakes as you."

"I... I... " his father faltered in saying anything, only staring at his son, truly seeing him for the first time. Willem was about to say more when the sound of broken glass could be heard.

Willem ran downstairs and met De Vries at the foot of the stairs.

"What's going on?"

De Vries shook his head. "It sounded like it came from the *voorhuis*."

"The front door, you think?" Willem asked as they made their way through the house. Shadowed faces watched them from their framed paintings on the walls.

"Or the small window beside it."

They hurried and reached the door to find that this was exactly what had happened. The little window had been smashed from the outside so an arm could reach inside and unlock the door. There was glass strewn all over the checkered floor.

"Where?" Willem asked as he glanced around.

"Your mother's parlor," De Vries whispered as he nudged Willem in the side. Without a word, they both headed down the short hallway that led into the Green Parlor. The noise of something clanking together could be heard before they reached it. De Vries was right.

As they entered the room, a small lamp revealed the intruder busy packing what valuables he could find into a large canvas bag. Silver candlesticks, Pieter's snuff-box, small pieces of art, even a painting had been stuffed in there.

"Yorov, you damned idiot," Willem exclaimed as he recognized the intruding thief.

Yorov turned, but it became clear he was half drunk as his swaying stance revealed the movement had been too abrupt.

"There you are, boy," he snickered. "Only came for what you owe me."

"I owe you nothing," Willem said.

"Who is this man?" De Vries asked. "Why has he been following you?"

"He's no one," Willem said, not hiding his smile. Willem had saved his family business; this creature was nothing more than bitter vermin.

"I'd watch that mouth if I were you," Yorov warned. "I should take your whole life from you. Teach you a lesson or two about wealth and power. See who could truly rise."

"Put down the valuables," De Vries said. His eyes never left the thief.

"These trinkets are nothing."

"Enough to pay for a drink so you don't have to steal from your daughters, I imagine," Willem said.

"Shut your mouth, you spoiled child," Yorov spat. "I'll take everything from you. I already have more worth without it," he roared and sprang at them.

Even with the knowledge of Yorov's ability, it came as a surprise to Willem. The gangly man lunged at De Vries first, the pulsating pink light encompassing his fist as he swung it at the servant. It didn't look like it had much force to it, but the flush and glowing force impacted hard with De Vries' face and sent the man flying to the floor. Willem barely registered his grunt of pain as the fist came back like a horizontal pendulum and hit him in the shoulder. The light burned as the force behind it pushed him so hard into the nearest wall that he was slammed back and to the floor as well. Willem groaned. Tried getting his breath back. Saw

De Vries getting up again. This time, the man was more prepared as he went for Yorov. Willem had never in his life seen the servant fight, but he was good at it. He ducked under Yorov's dangerous fist, landed a few punches himself and managed a solid kick in Yorov's sternum. It pushed the thief back a few steps. It dawned on Willem that Yorov's ability was not the same as Cornelia's, as hers gave her pure strength. This light burned with contact and weakened any opponent when struck.

Yorov regained his bearings, an impressive feat considering tonight's consumption of beer. De Vries didn't hesitate; he launched himself into a high kick, pivoting before his foot connected with Yorov's face. The thief roared in anger as he staggered sideways towards Willem, ready to strike De Vries again. Willem threw himself forward, crashing into Yorov's legs. It wasn't enough to topple him over, but it was enough to prevent him striking De Vries.

But Yorov shouted something in his anger, and the same light now came forth over his other hand. De Vries, who had paid attention to the first one, didn't have time to react as he was struck again. This time he was sent with his back first into the fireplace, cold ashes flying everywhere. Willem gathered his legs under him. How were they to get out of this? His ailing father was upstairs, and an old woman slept behind the kitchen. He had no doubt the crazed man would kill everyone in the house after this, and then take whatever he pleased.

Willem shouted words he couldn't understand himself as he hit Yorov in the back of the head. The man turned and sent his light-gilded fist back; the blow was so painful that Willem staggered backward a moment. That made Yorov laugh.

And then the lower part of his chest opened up, as De Vries came from behind and shoved a fire poker into the man. Willem stared in shock as the decorated metal pierced through Yorov's skin on his front side. For a moment they stared at each other, Yorov in pained shock as the foreign object paralyzed him. The light faded from his hands in a quick gust, and Willem noticed the little hook, the twined metal bent back to more easily move logs in the fire. It now protruded from Yorov's chest. Willem grabbed hold of it and pulled as De Vries pushed from the other side. With a strained yell from all three, the poker went clean through Yorov's body.

Willem and De Vries didn't stop to discuss anything. They simply acted. They shifted their grips and lifted the poker with the man that was impaled on it. Yorov howled in pain as the poker bored upward in his chest before they threw him towards the wall.

The man sank down under a window, which had no light to let in. The white curtain was stained with blood, as the man's death rattle was worse to listen to than Pieter's wheezing. There was a distinct gurgling coming from his lungs.

Willem and De Vries stood next to each other, breathing heavily from the strenuous fight. Willem felt the pain inflicted upon him, but couldn't take it in.

"I didn't think they could be defeated," he mumbled. He had been lucky with Cec, but Yorov had been alert and ready to defend himself despite his drinking. "I thought they were invincible."

"Who?" De Vries asked in his confusion.

Willem glanced at him, but the dying man on the floor drew his attention. He walked closer, seeing Yorov's blue eyes turn towards him as he came nearer. He was conscious enough in his dying moments.

"I'll tell you what, Yorov," Willem said as he crouched down beside the man. "I'll make you a promise and only because you told me some truths. You were right, you know. We only have our names, and they show our worth to the world. No one owes us anything, so if we want some-thing, we need to *take* it. I understand that now. There's no point in hiding who you are in this world. That's for the weak."

Yorov tried turning his head, but couldn't, so Willem grabbed his bearded chin with his blood-soaked hand and yanked it towards himself. It made a whimpering noise escape Yorov. A pitiful sound.

"You dreamed of people knowing your name, respecting it. And I'm going to promise you that. They *will* know your name all right, you foul old man. Weak, that's what you are in your all-consuming bitterness. When they hear your name, they will fear *me*... and they will blame you. Take that to your miserable, cold grave, why don't you?"

The whimper came again. It was all the mean-spirited thief could muster, before the gurgling stopped and Willem let go of his head as it sank back against the wall.

For a moment, he could only hear his own breathing. It was calm now. Steady and calm. Like he was himself. A shuffle of feet sounded behind him as De Vries shifted his position. Willem turned his head to see the man smiling. That same knowing smile he'd had all of Willem's life. But he understood it now as he realized what De Vries had always seen. His smile had never been in mockery; it had been in recognition.

18

The lights in Alice's house were out, all except one. It drew Willem like a beacon for the last few steps on the Rozen-straat as he neared the entrance. It made him smile, made him hope. So much had happened in the last few days that he'd not had time to go back, but now, in this stolen moment, he was glad he'd come at night. She worked long hours, didn't she? What with her obligations in the house-hold, nighttime was her own time to work with what gave her joy, what she was passionate about.

He smiled wider as he walked up the few steps to the front door and saw the scissors carved on the stone sign. Instead of knocking on the door, he leaned sideways over the railing, stretched out his arm and knocked on the green-tinted window. He saw a shadow move in the soft light in there and soon heard her approaching steps.

The door opened to reveal a curious face before she recognized him and a wide smile burst from her.

"Wim," she said as she stepped forward, put a hand on his neck and drew him into a kiss.

Willem lost his breath a moment. He had not expected this, but welcomed it nonetheless. Her soft, warm lips against his, searching and caressing at the same time. He had wished for that the moment she had climbed into the alcove with him the night they brought him there.

When she stepped back they both stared at the other in bewilderment for a moment; Cornelia in her surprise by her own actions and Willem in his wish for her not to stop.

"I'm sorry," she said, her voice incredulous with a soft hint of excitement as well. "I don't know why I did that."

"Don't be," he said and stepped closer. He raised his hand and stroked her hair behind her ear, let his fingers be entwined in the auburn locks he had longed to touch again. She tilted her chin up at the sensation, an invitation for him to lean in and kiss her back. She stepped closer as well and their arms went around each other. It was an embrace in the cold night that mirrored their shared night together in the alcove. Willem forgot everything in that moment. Every hard truth. Everything that was lost or regained to him. This was where he wanted to be, in Cornelia's arms. Somewhere where he was wanted as himself, no questions, no obligations. Only her and the need for her to be happy. The certainty that she wanted the same for him. Life could be good that way.

When he felt her shiver in his arms, he reluctantly broke the kiss and smiled at her.

"You're freezing."

They stepped inside the door and closed it. She was dressed in a long red dress, so deep red it bordered on brown. Her bodice was black, and it set off her hair that seemed lighter in comparison. Still, her good quality clothes were no match for the February night without wool and fur to keep her warm.

He followed her into her little sewing room. Her work table was covered by her latest projects, several ruffled cuffs for men to wear. She might wish to be a dressmaker one day, but for now, she took on the work she could. Her prices were likely more reasonable than a male tailor as well. She showed him her system, with shelves all around the room, fabrics for new projects, and clothes awaiting repair. It was all in a certain order depending on price and delivery. And yet, he sensed an urgency in her, like this was now more than her dream, more than working towards her goal.

"You have a lot more in here than the last time I saw it," he mentioned. The thought of his skirmish with Cec was no longer so harrowing in his mind after Yorov's attack.

"Oh," she said and ran a hand over a green dress that was slung over the back of a chair. "I've had to take on more."

"Why?"

"It doesn't have to worry you, Wim." She bit her lower lip and he wanted nothing more than to kiss it again.

"But now it does."

"Well, it's... some misfortune has befallen us lately. Fransiska has been taken by the magistrate."

"How unfortunate... "

"It's not a surprise really. Her drinking can match that of her father. Sometimes it makes her do stupid things."

"And her boy? Lieve?"

"Too young to provide much here. And Yorov is gone as well, not that he ever contributed much, that ingrate."

Willem only smiled.

"Anyway," Cornelia continued. "These are not your worries."

"They don't have to be yours either," Willem said and walked closer to her.

"What do you mean?" she said as she smiled and waited for him to reach her and take her smaller hands in his. Safe inside the comfort of a house, they were warm and soft, yet slightly calloused from her hard work. She gave a gentle squeeze in answer to his touch.

"Come away with me, Lia. I feel alive when I'm around you, like I can be who I want to, not who I am."

She gave a soft laugh. "I'm sure you don't need me for that?"

"I do. I think you matter more to me than anything else. Will you come?"

"Come where?"

"To live out the rest of your life with me. You don't have to do this work. I sold the tulip. You don't ever have to work again."

"But Catharijn saw the end of the tulips. And she was right." She had been. The authorities had put an end to the craze that had spread like a burning fever through the population. The crash of the tulip market had rendered many a Dutchman destitute over the past few days. It had become a turmoil many chose not to live through.

"I moved quickly, thanks to your grandmother's gift."

"So someone else lost their money in your stead?" Cornelia asked, head tilted to the side as she tried to fit those pieces together.

"It is the cost of dealing in such a market."

"I... " Cornelia shook her head. "I... "

"What say you?"

"Can't you come here? Join our life. It may be different, but the things you'll see... "

"I can't. I promised my father I'd look after his business." Willem would simply be doing it on his own terms. He couldn't leave the business now. He had taken over in his own right, not his brother's, and he had such plans. He wanted her by his side while he saw these plans come to fruition. "Will you come with me? I'm sure your grandmother won't object."

"I don't think she will, no, but Oma is getting older. Soon, I'll have to take care of her. And what about everyone else here?"

"They don't have to be your responsibility, Lia. You can live your own life. I will provide for them of course." *It would be no trouble*, he thought, as his new and improved business was already showing signs of growth. All the desperate merchants now trying to save themselves from their worthless tulips also helped. And it would be a small price to pay for having this extraordinary woman as his wife. She would be marrying up, but she could learn the ways of his world with ease.

"But Wim, that's not the issue," Cornelia said, the joy in her eyes fading to worry now. "I don't wish to *pay* for their comfort. I wish to *be* their comfort, like they are mine."

The pain in Willem's chest from his desperate time in the ice-cold canal had subsided quickly, thanks to Alice's remedy. But as Cornelia's hands let go of his and her words got through to him, he felt the ache return. This time, Alice would not be able to heal him.

19

Willem walked through the front door of the house in the Keizersgracht, relieved to be out of the fog that had descended upon the city. A few minutes later and he would have had trouble finding his way home. The fog had felt colder than the icy waters of the canal that had been part of changing his life a few weeks ago. Of course, he knew that was only his imagination. With time, he was forgetting how cold it had really been.

"Oh, Master Willem," Hendrika said, relief in her voice. "So glad to see you home and safe. This blasted fog could send any man toppling into a canal on a night like this."

Willem only smiled as she took his cloak to put it away. "How is Father doing?"

"A little better," the old woman answered, but her hands wringing her apron told Willem she didn't want to acknowledge the truth. They could afford doctors now, but it had been too late to save Pieter de Meer from the illness that would no doubt claim him eventually.

"And dinner?"

"I'll heat it up for you. De Vries and the boy have eaten.

I think the little one is coming around quite well to his new home."

"Good. Anything else?"

"Yes. A visitor."

"Really? At this hour?"

"Yes. I showed her into the Green Parlor."

Willem entered the parlor which had been restored to his mother's comfort again. There were no traces left in there of Yorov's end. No blood, no ashes. All the things he'd tried to take were now put back where they belonged.

Catharijn van Heuvel stood in the middle of the room, dressed in a striking gown of deep brown and gray brocade, while a golden curl had yet again escaped from under her cap.

"I hear your tulip sale went well," she said after their greeting.

Willem nodded. "Thanks to you and your...foresight."

Catharijn looked around nervously, despite knowing they were alone. "I'm sorry I kept our knowledge of each other a secret that day. No one but Andries knows about my situation. However, all he knows for now is that I am to marry a merchant's son."

"No need for apologies."

"They will know eventually, but I didn't think that the time or place."

"Understandable."

She clasped her hands together, the nervous gesture mimicking that of Hendrika.

"I've come to ask for news," she said after a moment.

"News?"

"About your favor to me. To arrange for our engagement to be broken."

"Ah," Willem said and walked past her, and through the door that led back to his father's old study. "I'm afraid I have none," he said over his shoulder as he heard her scramble to keep up, the rustle of her skirts as she walked through the hallway. "Father is rather adamant that an agreement is to be kept."

"What?"

Willem opened the door and strode inside, glad to see that Hendrika had stoked the fire until his arrival. He walked past the desk to the small cabinet made of teak. He opened it to find his father's little collection of fine spirits but chose the brandy, his own favorite.

"I thought your father was indisposed," Catharijn said as she took in the room. She, like so many others, had never been in there before. The large desk took up most of the space, the walls covered with bookshelves. Near the window stood a smaller desk for whichever employee was helping his father at the time. Papers and documents dominated both desk surfaces now as Willem was using most of his time learning about new business ventures these days.

"He is unwell but strong of mind," Willem told her. "Brandy? Or do you prefer wine?"

Catharijn shook her head at the offer, and Willem filled a glass for himself.

"But I thought... " her words trailed away from her and she looked down a moment. "Will you hate me if I run away?"

Willem shrugged and smiled.

"Why would you? Your father and brothers lost a substantial amount of their fortune because of their tulip speculation, I hear. I'm sure they rely on this union. You didn't tell them about the crash, did you?"

"No," she whispered.

"Wanted them to suffer a little for arranging your life for you?"

She didn't meet his eye, and he knew he was right. Anger had stopped her from helping them, and guilt would keep her away from the Rozenstraat now. Which was just as well. Without Cornelia, he had need of Catharijn.

"How is life in the Rozenstraat, by the way?" he asked, hoping despite the pain, that she would mention Cornelia. Was she happy without him?

"Odd. Fransiska is in prison, her boy and Yorov are missing, and only last night, Arend was arrested as well."

"Your lover's brother?"

She nodded. "Yes, for no apparent reason. They hauled him away as he returned home."

Willem clicked his tongue and drained the glass.

"Strange indeed. Perhaps you shouldn't associate with such people? What would your father say? Besides, people can easily be taken away by the guards. And they can, of course, easily be freed from them." He put the empty glass on the desk and went over to the fireplace where he found a log to put on the weakening flames.

Catharijn's silence behind him filled the room like an echo of despair as understanding hit her. Her man would be safe, but not his loved ones. That would not make them stronger together. In the end, he would resent the trouble she brought upon them.

"Don't worry about your secret," Willem said as he turned back to her. She looked beaten then, her lovely face sad, though he knew her blue eyes watched him despite their downcast appearance. "It's safe with me. Any children born with it will also be safe. You have my word." He didn't only want to keep her secret, he *wanted* her secret as well.

"I suppose I do," she said as she understood his full meaning. "For what it's worth."

At that time, his father's old servant chose to manifest in the doorway. Either he sensed these things, or he listened at doors. Willem didn't care. He'd come to under-stand the man's worth: his loyalties and talents.

"Ah, De Vries," Willem said. "Would you please escort

Ms. Van Heuvel home? The fog outside might lead her astray, and it makes for no place for a young lady to be out on her own."

"Yes, Mynheer," De Vries said and nodded to Catharijn. "If you'll wait by the door a moment. I need a word with Mynheer de Meer."

Catharijn nodded and walked past Willem without giving him a second glance. She would go home, thankful they even still had one after the folly of the men in her family. Her mother still resided there and still needed to reside there. Catharijn would go home and help with that.

"Your father is strong of mind, huh?" De Vries said as they heard Catharijn's steps disappear down the hall.

"Can't go against his will, now can I? So, you listen at doors?"

De Vries shrugged and leaned against the smaller desk.

"How else am I supposed to do my job?"

"And how is that job going?"

"That's what I wanted to ask you about," De Vries said as a red-headed boy came running into the office.

"De Vries," he shouted. "I cut myself." He held out a simple dagger to the man, polished bone-handle with no decorations. He was bleeding from a small cut on his finger.

"Then you did it wrong, and not the way I showed you. Try again. And don't go changing my dagger into something else either."

"But—"

"No buts. And don't ever enter Mynheer de Meer's office without permission, Lieve. You hear me?"

The boy nodded his head as he looked down.

Willem watched with a smile as he walked out, murmuring an apology to Willem on his way.

"A dagger?" Willem asked.

"He needs to be able to protect himself. He works in a fine house now. Servants like that earn a little more money, and some folk will try and rob him sooner rather than later."

"He has other weapons... "

"Yes, I've come to understand that," De Vries said, still a little hesitant to know about it as well as take in someone with such an otherworldly talent. He had not forgotten the death of Yorov. "But if he's not supposed to show that to everyone, then he needs other means to defend himself."

"Very well. I trust your judgment in this regard."

De Vries made no comment to that. They both knew that he knew best.

"So, what was your question?"

"What am I to do with him? Besides teaching him how to survive?"

Willem breathed in, the smell of smoke filling his nose as he grabbed his glass again.

"You're to teach the boy the most important thing he'll ever learn."

"And that is?"

"Loyalty."

Willem walked back to find the brandy bottle as De Vries left to follow his fiancée home. Maybe it was just as well *The Filomena* had gone down? It had been the final nail in the coffin of the family business meant for Geert. But that shipwreck had opened up new possibilities for Willem himself. The world was, after all, full of them. You only had to make proper use of the means that crossed your path to make your wants come true.

EPILOGUE

Amsterdam, March 1647

The bite of the cold air felt like several slaps in the face, especially every time Cornelia changed directions. The day she would see Willem de Meer again, for the first time in a decade, was a cold and freezing day, much like the first time she had laid eyes on him.

She still remembered the sweet young man who'd saved her younger brother that night by risking his own life. His smile, so handsome when he allowed himself to be happy; the thick hair with the deep brown color, so soft to the touch; the friendly blue eyes that tried desperately to hold his true self back in this world. She had treasured their short time together. Could remember it so vividly all these years later, mostly because that man had disappeared in what she had later pieced together to be a mix of guilt, loyalty, and pride.

"Are you all right, Lia?" came the hoarse voice of Annetje, the beggar woman.

Cornelia looked down at her own gloved hand, coin still between her fingers.

"Yes, I'm sorry. Here you go. How are you doing anyway?"

"Can't complain, can't complain," Annetje chanted. She looked like an overstuffed bread roll in her various blankets over her patched-up cloak. Cornelia had helped her with that, but that had been a few years ago. Annetje was not affiliated with their community, but as a beggar with her own connections throughout Amsterdam, they had crossed paths. Especially after Cornelia had been given the mantle as a leader after her Oma's death. "You look like you've seen a ghost though," Annetje added.

"Come now, Annetje," Cornelia said and smiled despite the danger she knew she was in. "Haven't you learned anything from us over the years? There aren't many ghosts."

Annetje shrugged and a lock of her steel-gray hair fell out from under her hood. "All I say is I know what I know."

"Is something wrong, Mama?"

Cornelia turned to her daughter, Alice. Her little girl's bright face looked at her with worry and the green eyes of Cornelia's late husband. She took Alice's hand in hers. There was no point in lying to her. The child had inherited her father's gift, or Oma's, or both. It didn't matter. But with an empath as a daughter, Cornelia's deep worry could not be hidden. She straightened up and pulled Alice closer as she put an arm around the girl's shoulder. The harbor was teeming with people. Although the winter prevented many sea travels, there were a few places that were safe even at this time of year. Vendors went about, shouting out their special offers, stallholders did the same, though in a less mobile fashion. Other people milled about, meeting people, trading, working on the ships. Dogs barked, and seagulls screamed. And despite being hidden in the middle of this crowd, Cornelia felt exposed.

"You see those men?" she asked her daughter. She didn't dare to point. Every gifted affiliate in the city knew to stay away from them.

"Who?" Alice asked, her eyes darting across the ever-moving people around them. She quickly found the right group as her mother described them to her. The thin and gray-haired servant of the De Meer household, De Vries, known to every affiliate as a man you ran away from if you wanted to escape unscathed. The red-headed young man named Lieve, once such a sweet boy who'd been eager to show off his ability, and shy around the dinner table. The fat man, Pieter van Linden, who worked for his cousin, a once rich man himself who now ran a section of the company they all feared. There were other men around them as well where they stood. They were all greeting a business acquaintance from a nearby ship. The newcomers were all dressed in thick fur-trimmed cloaks that kept them nice and warm in the cold, but Cornelia did not know these men. They had joined during her time in Oma's homeland. She had promised to take the old woman there a few years ago as she had become ill and wished to spend her last days where she was born. Cornelia sighed as she forced herself to look again at the man she no longer knew. Willem de Meer had aged well. He still looked the same, though there was a distinct authority to his manner now. It could certainly be seen in the way the men around him listened to him.

"Are they the ones...?" Alice began to ask but stopped herself.

Cornelia nodded and felt her daughter squeeze her hand for comfort.

"You'd best learn this now, Alice," she said, hardening her voice to get through it. "Those men are not our friends. They hunt people like us to use us for their own gain. It's how they've become so powerful. Whatever you do in life, my girl, you stay away from the Yorov Shipping and Wholesale Company."

"You mark your mother's words, girl," Annetje chimed in from her chosen spot on the ground. "People who cross them... well, they do not fare well."

Alice nodded solemnly, but Cornelia was glad they were leaving the city that very day. Amsterdam was no longer a safe place for any community of the gifted. She knew the Yorov Company had even begun searching outside the city now. Never before had anyone used their abilities for such devious behaviors: to earn money and gain power. And they all owed their allegiance to the man who had once saved her from such a threat.

Cornelia forgot herself a moment, as Lieve and a pair of other young men left the group to go tend to whatever errand they had been given. Next to Willem de Meer stood a boy, not much older than her Alice. She could see the resemblance between father and son, even from the distance. The boy looked up at his father with undeniable pride. Cornelia had learned from those in the various communities that Catharijn had borne him three children over the years, two boys and a girl. Whether they took after their mother was a well-kept secret, but Cornelia suspected Willem had not been that lucky. The company he had founded under another name than his own, an oddity in itself as he had seemed to dislike the old bastard, had never been ahead of deals in that way. They had always managed to push their way in instead.

Cornelia's thoughts distracted her enough for the young De Meer to yank his father's ruffled cuff and point at her, asking a question. Her heart in her throat, she realized the boy had noticed her looking. Willem turned to see where his boy was pointing and froze as he recognized her. For a mere moment, she had wondered if he would. But her unmistakable long auburn hair hung over her shoulder, free from her cloak and the hood she now wished she had pulled over her head.

His face was blank, but his disregard for anything else told her he knew her. His eyes searched hers, looking for an answer to something. Then he noticed Alice by her side, the girl's hair color telling him what he needed to know about her. Cornelia caught herself wondering what he was thinking though. Who had she married? Was the child like her mother? What ability had she inherited? What life had Cornelia led without him? A pang hit her as she thought about that night when she had chosen her community first. She knew now it had been the right thing to do, but it still hurt a little. She still grieved for who he had been and what could have been.

One of the men approached Willem, distracting him by asking something. Cornelia didn't hesitate.

"We need to move," she told her daughter and pulled her with her into the nearest side street, narrow and dark. Alice was too surprised to resist, and then too overcome with her mother's emotions to ask why.

Cornelia dared to look out from her shaded hiding place to see Willem's eyes searching the harbor around him, but he hadn't seen where she had gone. *Nor will he ever,* she thought as her Oma's homeland awaited her and Alice in the spring. Until then, they would stay with friends farther north. Amsterdam was too dangerous for them. Even her. She held on tight to her daughter as they found a longer and safer way to their ship.

Sign up for G.K. Lund's newsletter to get news and behind the scenes updates as well as a fantasy starter collection.

Get it here:
https://my.gklundwrites.com/books-and-news

Author's note

The tulip fever is an actual historical event that took place in the Netherlands in the17[th] century. People would bid outrageous sums of money for the flowers, which only blooms for about a week. I agree they are beautiful, but I would not sell my home for one.

The tulip fever is considered an example of an economic bubble, much like some people predict today's cryptocurrencies to be. As of yet, none of them have plummeted as fast as the tulips did in 1637. They were deemed worthless by the authorities overnight, and many a Dutchman became destitute just as fast.

I first came across this historical event when I read *The Black Tulip* by Alexandre Dumas in my teens (though that story is actually set after the tulipmania itself). When I planned the story of the origins of the Yorov Company, somehow it ended up entwined with the mania that surrounded these flowers. This fictional company, which looms in the shadows in my other books, encompasses a great greed for power and control, and the greed that followed the tulips during this time is a fitting symbol for that.

G.K.Lund is an independent fantasy author with a love of old stories and folklore; anything that's dark, weird and wonderful. It's a good thing then that G.K. is based roughly somewhere in the realm of Scandiwegia where old myths are plentiful.

G.K. has a background in archaeology (dirty nails and all) and will probably have to put an archeologist into a story one day. Until then, potty-mouthed and kickass characters with other jobs will have to face high stakes and save the day.

Connect with G.K. Lund
https://gklundwrites.com

Urban Fantasy

<u>Atlantis Outcasts:</u>

Malicious Magic #1

Curses in the Light #2

Rebels and Traitors #3

<u>The Ashdale Reaper Series:</u>

Deadly Awakening #1

Grave Intent #2

Dance of Death #3

Revenants of Life #4

Primal Powers (short story)

Hidden Fire (novelette)

Paranormal Romance

<u>The Ashport Mender Series:</u>

Outsider #1

Persistence #2

Dissonance #3

Convergence #4

Historical Fantasy

Avarice

Northern Quill Press

ISBN: 978-82-93663-11-9

www.gklundwrites.com

Cover design by Damonza

Edited by Megan Easley-Walsh and N. Hall

Avarice / G.K. Lund, 1st. ed.

 Formatted with Vellum